# POLITICS Suck

Paperback ISBN: 979-8-9892805-2-0

Ebook ISBN: 979-8-9892805-3-7

Library of Congress Control Number: 2024919581

First Edition 2024

# POLITICS *Suck*

## *A Wellsprings Rivals Romance*

# ROSEMARIE DILLON

EVEREST
ROSE PRESS

This story contains content that may be troubling to some readers, including, but not limited to, death by suicide, attempted suicide, homophobia, hate speech, gun violence, and cultural whitewashing.

No deaths occur on-page.

If you or a loved one are struggling, please contact the Suicide and Crisis Lifeline. Call or text "988" to speak to someone today. You are not alone.

*To those who have ever been made to feel less than by their loved ones. You are valued and this world is a better place having you in it.*

*To my family, thank you for never making me feel that way.*

# CHAPTER 1

## Clay

Clay Emerson looked out at the flashing lights and waving rainbow flags in the crowd. A young man in the front row had single-handedly stopped the debate with a scream. He held an oak-tag poster asking Clay to marry him and several audience members squealed in delight. Clay wasn't sure how his mayoral campaign could elicit such declarations. His rallies had all but turned into a Pride parade since publicly announcing his homosexuality.

A voice rang out through the speaker system. "If I may?" Clay blinked at the poster before turning back to the man across from him. His opponent scowled from behind his podium, adjusting his necktie. Sebastian Rivera, opposing mayoral candidate, cleared his throat and continued to drone on about taxes.

Clay promptly tuned it out. He'd been busy daydreaming about the Halloween weekend. His campaign had only just begun, and he was already exhausted. Clay intended on trolling some gay bars in the neighboring town to let off steam. Preparation for the campaign had been brutal. Late nights, lonely takeout dinners, and a cold bed awaited him in his condo. No, tonight he needed a pretty boy to kiss and suck the soul out of his dick. He felt his cock twitch at the thought. So, he focused on the one sure-fire thing to kill a boner… Sebastian's voice.

Clay yawned discreetly after fielding another question. Sebastian rebutted. *God, he's long winded. Get to the point, man.* Clay found a more relaxed position on the podium and studied his foe.

Sebastian would be attractive if his mouth was sealed shut. His skin was leather brown and supple, crinkling slightly at his eyes and mouth. Clay had to admit, he had magnificent hair. His hair was coiffed in a stylish wave, with bits of gray peppering his temples. Clay's eyes wandered, watching Sebastian's arms move as he gestured with his hands. The suit clung tightly to his biceps and shoulders. The jacket molded nicely to his abdomen, but the tailoring was all wrong on the top. It was as if a gorilla was playing dress up.

Sebastian Rivera was seriously *jacked*. Clay swallowed around a lump in his throat, wondering what the hell lurked beneath that suit. It was about then that he realized silence was hanging in the air. Sebastian glared at him incredulously.

"I'm sorry, please repeat the question," Clay murmured into the microphone. Feedback screeched in the speakers as the moderator answered.

"What are your thoughts on budgeting?"

"Simple. We need to allocate more funds to schools. Our teachers direly need supplies, fair pay, and the arts department is lacking in extracurriculars. I'd also like to allot a stipend for anti-bullying curriculum." A quiet came over the crowd. Clay had grown up here, gone to the only high school in town. They knew his history. "I propose repurposing funds from the casino to achieve this." Murmurs rose from the crowd. "This would help avoid raising taxes. The casino is thriving and not in any danger of bankruptcy. Reallocating funds to our children's future is well worth the risk." Saying the words "our children," made him wince. That was a sticky situation he'd banish from his mind.

Sebastian raised a single eyebrow and sighed into his microphone.

"What Mr. Emerson fails to understand is that the casino is the largest currency generator in Wellsprings. A reduction from their taxed revenue could have an adverse effect on the economy." The condescending tone in Sebastian's voice sharply poked at Clay's thin patience.

"Actually, Mr. Rivera, my team has been working tirelessly to ensure the casino's online visibility, and we've been closely collaborating with the owners to specifically target big spenders through digital advertising. The casino is already seeing the effects. Profits have skyrocketed." Whispers of approval floated in the space between the two men. Clay smirked and lowered the boom. "If anything, this will create more jobs."

Gasps and excitement erupted around them. Sebastian's eyebrows shot up, his mouth slightly agape. Wellspring's unemployment rate had reached nearly seven percent. It was a huge point of contention in this election. As quickly as Sebastian's shock appeared, it vanished, his face returning to immovable stone. The moderator took that opportunity to close the debate portion of the evening and have each candidate give closing statements.

The bodyguards escorted both Clay and Sebastian off stage once their speeches were over. Jade, Clay's lead guard, kept a firm hand between his shoulder blades. She guided them to a line of waiting cars. Sebastian's team clustered around their vehicles, speaking in urgent whispers. Sebastian caught Clay's gaze despite his team's chattering.

He stepped beside Clay and Jade wedged herself in between them, in full on defense mode.

"Can you call off your attack dog?" Sebastian crossed his arms, his muscles straining against the fabric. Clay swallowed and placed his palm on Jade's shoulder.

"Jade, it's fine." She looked over her shoulder and raised a single dark eyebrow before stepping aside. Sebastian stuffed his hands into his pants pockets and scowled at Clay. Clay couldn't help noticing that Sebastian had already undone his tie. It hung limply around his neck, the first two buttons of his shirt collar open. Soft, curly chest hair peeked out from the opening. Clay focused back on Sebastian's angry face.

"To what do I owe this pleasure, Mr. Rivera?"

"The casino," he said gruffly, all sense of professionalism stripped. "How did you get them to work with you? I couldn't even get a meeting with Stella Simmons."

"Just some perseverance," Clay shrugged his shoulders and mimicked his rival, shoving his hands in his pants pockets. "I knew Stella from the city council meetings. She was often in attendance. You would, of course, know that if you worked on the council."

It was still a sore spot with Clay—Sebastian had simply announced he was going to run for mayor out of the blue. Coming from money, Sebastian was given every opportunity in life. Clay, on the other hand, had to bust his ass to announce his candidacy. Since graduating high school, he'd worked closely with all the city council members. He knew all the town's shop owners by name. He never missed a school budget meeting. He always volunteered at the rec center. He knew how important it was to put his best foot forward, because at the end of the day, some backwoods, close-minded conservative would look at

Clay and only see a gay man. A gay man who, sadly, in many people's eyes, didn't even deserve the right to marry... much less exist.

"That was a low blow tonight, Emerson. You never spoke about this plan of yours before." Sebastian's voice was practically a growl. Jade snapped to attention and edged closer to Clay, signaling him with her eyes to end the conversation.

"Well, I intend to win, Mr. Rivera. I refrained from mentioning the plan previously as I had nothing concrete to promise the people of Wellsprings. Now, if you'll excuse me, I have another engagement to attend."

Jade opened the car door, and they smooshed into the back seat of the Toyota Corolla. The town insisted on providing cars for the two candidates, determined to treat the small-town mayoral race as a big event. It was the most excitement the town had seen since the late mayor Hubert's funeral. Clay appreciated the sentiment, but maybe they should ask for a car with a bigger back seat. He quickly calculated the cost and inwardly sighed. There wasn't enough money in the budget to allow for anything else.

Clay watched in envy as Sebastian climbed into the back of his Lincoln Town Car. Clay had assumed Sebastian's parents provided it. No doubt unwilling to see the heir to the Rivera fortune climb out of a Toyota. Clay ground his teeth, seeing Sebastian's perky ass disappear into luxury. *Just let him have his fun pretending to be important. That election is mine.*

# Chapter 2

## Sebastian

His biceps throbbed under the strain of pounding the punching bag into oblivion. After any encounter with Clay Emerson, Sebastian would feel the supreme urge to beat the ever-living fuck out of something... or bake. *Cute little pompous bastard.* He roundhouse kicked the bag before stalking off angrily to the showers. His phone chirped from his pocket, and he rolled his eyes, tossing it into his gym locker before stripping out of his sweat-soaked gym clothes.

The text was most likely from his father. One from his mother would undoubtedly follow. *Ding.* Sebastian huffed in annoyance and stepped under the hot shower spray, putting his parents out of his mind for a moment. He'd spied them in the debate crowd even after asking them *not* to come. But, true to form, Victor and Essie Rivera wouldn't dare miss an opportunity to publicly support their son in everything he does.

Sebastian could only imagine his old man turning purple when Clay had announced his coalition with the casino. A smile wormed its way onto his face. Victor had been working for months to get a foot in the door, but that wily Clay weaseled his way in through his connections from the council. Sebastian had told his parents he should be more involved with the community boards if they had wanted him to run. But no, surely their money would earn him a spot. Sebastian was beside himself when they proved to be right.

After letting the hot water unwind his muscles, he slung a towel around his waist and checked his phone. Three missed calls and five texts. All asking where he was and why he wasn't at the party yet. Sebastian tossed his phone into his gym bag and pulled the garment bag from the locker's hangar. Another stupid benefit party. Another stupid tux. He unzipped the bag, and a bright red ornate mask greeted him.

A masquerade. How gauche. Sebastian scoffed and pulled out the red tux. Leave it to his parents to turn a Halloween party into a masquerade benefit gala. Rolling his eyes, he dressed in a robotic manner, tossing the mask back in the garment bag.

"Bas?" A deep baritone voice rang out in the empty locker room.

"All good, Marc," Sebastian sighed, rounding the corner to see his bodyguard on alert at the room's entrance. Marc's thick shoulders loosened, and he smiled good-naturedly, turning to lead the way out of the gym. Marc was once a shortstop for Wellsprings High School, on the fast track to a full ride scholarship until he tore his ACL. Since graduating, he'd taken odd jobs, anything utilizing his strength. When Sebastian had heard that his best friend from high school had been assigned as a bodyguard, he was beyond pleased.

"So how many times did your parents call you? They called me four times while I was taking a leak." Marc opened the car door for me, signaling the driver to start up the engine.

"Three calls, five texts. They're incorrigible." Sebastian slid into the back seat and pulled his mask from the bag. "I mean, look at this thing. What happened to a normal benefit event? No one takes us seriously because of this frivolous bullshit."

"Ah, they love to do it up. The people who attend are all rich, anyway. That's just how it goes for them." Marc shrugged his big shoulders and relaxed back into the plush seat. Sebastian harrumphed and scowled out the window. He found it ridiculous to even have been assigned a bodyguard. He was running for mayor in a small town, not the presidency.

The party was being hosted at one of his mother's friend's residences a few towns away. The car pulled up to a large brownstone, music thumping, drunken couples dancing on the lawn in their masquerade outfits. Sebastian looked down at his mask, smoothing out the red, orange, and yellow feathers. He snapped the thing onto his face, the pointy beak hooked over his nose. He looked at Marc, who promptly burst out laughing.

"I'm going to kill her," Sebastian ground out between his teeth. He flung the door open and stalked through the waltzing partygoers. He stomped up the stairs, his mother greeting him with a hug.

"Oh, Sebby, I was so worried when you didn't answer." She was dressed as what Sebastion assumed was a snowy owl princess.

"Mom," he pointed a finger at his own mask, "what the hell is this supposed to be? I look ridiculous."

"You're a phoenix, dear. We all went as majestic birds." She gestured toward Victor, who had a similar mask to Sebastian's, only it was in the colors of a bald eagle. Victor caught his eyes, his jovial face quickly souring. *Can't wait to scream about the casino, huh Dad?* Essie placed a hand on his arm, calling back his attention. "Sebby, I wanted to introduce you to someone." A dangerous glint in her eye put Sebastian on guard. His mother took him by the hand and dragged him through the brownstone, pausing to allow Sebastian to thank the host for the use of their home.

"Cassidy, this is my son," Essie pushed Sebastian forward. He stood much too close to a thin blonde woman, dressed as some sort of ice princess in a puffy gown. Sebastian glared daggers at his mom before putting space between him and Cassidy. He shook her hand and introduced himself. Cassidy looked him over appreciatively.

"Lovely to meet you, but if you would excuse us, I need to speak to my mother," Sebastian must've had his smile screwed on a bit too tight because Cassidy quirked an eyebrow as he ushered his mom to a private drawing room.

"Oh, what is it now? We should be mingling."

"Again, you're doing this? I already told you and Dad—"

"Sebastian, please. You cannot be a bachelor your entire life. Your dad and I want you to be happy." When Essie was angry, her accent became more apparent. But as soon as it appeared, she'd tamped it down. Since moving to Wellsprings, Victor had been insistent that their family should bleach their Puerto Rican heritage from their lives in order to succeed. Victor was now a prominent landowner with millions of dollars in assets. He asserted that his light skin and "white people talk" were what led him to greatness. Not his smart real estate decisions and entrepreneurial mind.

Because Sebastian's skin was darker, like his mother's, Victor was especially ruthless in keeping his speech whitewashed. Sebastian couldn't even speak Spanish, much to the shock of his colleagues.

"I know you think Dad can control our lives, but he can't. You know why I won't date that white girl out there."

"I do not control your lives. I simply protect them," a rumbling voice joined them. Victor closed the door behind him with a deafening latch. He slowly approached them with the calculating eyes of a predator. "Where have you been, Sebastian? You're supposed to be mingling with the guests... especially after that debacle with the casino." His voice turned to ice at the word casino. "Have you met Cassidy Whipple? It's about time you thought about having children. Cassidy comes from a prestigious family. She has wonderful genes."

"No." Sebastian's voice rang out. "And you know why." Essie's eyes widened and Victor's jaw clenched. Victor prattled on about Cassidy's white pedigree and monetary value, but Sebastian had stopped listening, rage pounding in his ears. He pushed past his father, who roughly grabbed him by the arm. The two were at a standoff, glaring at each other until Victor finally loosened his grip and Sebastian jerked away.

He burst out of the brownstone, visibly fuming. Marc was in the crowd, always vigilantly scanning for potential threats. When he spied Sebastian clomping down the stairs, he moved closer. Sebastian sharply shook his head and Marc nodded in understanding, blending back into the crowd.

Sebastian stalked down the sidewalk, quickly entering the downtown area. The bars were crowded, people in costume filtering in and out of doors. He typically avoided crowded areas, not interested in making small talk. But he came upon a bar that gave him pause. It was crowded, but less so. The sign above filtered a rainbow of light down on his face. With the anger still rushing through his blood, he took a deep breath and slipped inside.

# Chapter 3

## Clay

Clay arranged his fake breasts. *How do women wear bras every day?* He fluffed out his wig and sipped his martini.

"Jesus, the bathroom line was insane." Jade plopped onto the stool beside Clay, her dalmatian ears bobbing.

"Sorry, *darling,* can't relate." Clay slipped his drink again and smiled. He loved getting into character on Halloween. Clay's Cruella drag was on point and he was getting a lot of looks. He'd already received drinks from a Michael Meyers, a scarecrow, and a wizard. They weren't what Clay was looking for, so he'd chatted a moment and moved on. He'd been scanning the crowd from the bar all night while Jade flirted with any cute person who passed by.

Clay's attention turned to the door as a group entered. Several fresh faces immediately crowded around the bar. He could see a hulking man wander in behind them, smartly dressed in a blood red tuxedo with an intricate feathered phoenix mask covering his face. The phoenix looked around the space, presumably searching for an empty seat to occupy. Clay followed his gaze as he sipped his drink. The phoenix's eyes eventually landed on him. Clay choked on the olive he'd been sucking as the man made a beeline toward him. More accurately, the empty stool to his left.

Clay frantically searched the crowd for Jade, suddenly feeling exposed without his appointed guard. He finally laid eyes on her, sandwiched between a male and female couple, taking turns making out with them. *Traitor.* The phoenix sat on the stool with a heavy sigh, calling for the bartender, even having the gall to snap his fingers at her. Clay bristled. It was most decidedly *not sexy* to be rude to a bartender, or anyone working in food service, for that matter. Clay screwed a smile onto his face and took up his Cruella play-act.

"Oh, *Darling*, are you in such desperate need of a drink? I'm sure Roxy will assist you shortly."

The phoenix's eyes dragged themselves over to look at Clay. He cleared his throat and looked down at his clasped hands on the bar top.

"You're right. That was rude... been a long day." He put his hands under his mask and scrubbed before putting the mask back in place. Clay felt disappointed he couldn't see under it. The phoenix's beak nodded at Clay's drink. "What are you drinking, Cruella?"

Clay straightened his spine, fingering the glass's rim. A small thrill raced through him at the thought of escaping to the bathroom with this guy.

"Dirty vodka martini." Clay pushed his glass toward him, offering the small bit of liquid left. "Sorry, no olive." Clay showed him the olive cradled between his teeth before sucking it back into his mouth. The man's jaw tightened, and Clay swore he could see him swallow. In one swift motion, never breaking eye contact, the phoenix threw back the martini.

"Hm, good. I'll get you another for your trouble." The phoenix grabbed Roxy's attention, remarkably politely. She quickly brought their drinks over and the phoenix slipped a hundred-dollar bill across the bar top. She snatched it up, winked at him, and sauntered off to assist other patrons. There was something about how rich people flaunted their money that rubbed Clay the wrong way. Clay rose an eyebrow at the man and dropped his Cruella voice for a moment.

"I can buy my own drink. How much do I owe you?" The phoenix tilted his head in confusion. Clay unclasped his dalmatian patterned clutch for cash, but the man put his hand on Clay's.

"I don't need your money. But I know what you can give me." The phoenix scooted closer on the bar stool, pushed his mask further up on his face, and took hold of Clay's chin. Clay opened his mouth to make a snarky comment, but the man's plush lips swallowed his words. Clay groaned into his mouth and clutched his lapels. He'd kissed a lot of men, but none made him feel like his skin was on fire before. The phoenix slipped his tongue between Clay's pliable lips and tangled with his own. The man's free arm snaked around Clay's waist and jerked him against his solid chest.

As quickly as it'd started, the phoenix pulled away. Clay knew his cheeks were flushed and lips bee-stung. He fluttered his eyelids for a moment to catch his breath. The phoenix cursed softly, and straightened his spine, waiting for Clay to refocus his gaze.

Once Clay's hands stopped shaking, he looked back at the man. The phoenix grinned, olive between his teeth. Clay hadn't realized he'd stolen it, too wrapped up in the taste of his mouth. The phoenix crushed the olive and chewed, tossing back his fresh martini.

"Thanks. I love olives," he purred. Clay stammered for a heartbeat before Jade interrupted and yanked on his arm.

"So, this nice couple wants me to leave with them. Are you okay to stay by yourself? Or should I call you an Uber?"

"I, uh..." He turned back to his left and found an empty chair. The man's glass was drained and all the olives had been dumped into Clay's drink. His shoulders drooped, and he picked up his still full martini. "You go ahead. I'll grab some dinner with Roxy when her shift ends."

"Okay, you nut." She kissed his temple and gave him a little squeeze. "Call me if you need me." Jade gleefully sauntered out of the bar. Clay sighed, spun his drink on the bar top, then turned his attention back to the crowd, determined to find a willing participant to take care of the erection beneath Cruella's dress.

# Chapter 4

## Zamboni

A squirrel scurried across a quivering tree branch. It edged ever closer to the house, testing its limits. Once the squirrel touched its paw to the grass, Zamboni was on the defensive, barking in his angry bark, one he rarely used. The squirrel heeded his message, shot up the tree and hopped the fence to the neighbor's yard. Zamboni sneezed in triumph.

"Who was it now, Zambo? Did you protect us from the squirrel invaders?" A human popped his head over the fence. Zamboni wagged his tail rapidly. He liked this fence-human. He always gave him cookies. Zamboni approached, and the man shoved a dog biscuit through a small hole in the wooden fence. Zamboni snatched it up and swallowed it without chewing. The human patted his head and went on his way, shoving papers into a metal box on a pole. Zambo stood on his hind legs, resting his front paws on the fence to watch the fence-human retreat down the sidewalk to continue his paper depositing ritual.

Ensuring fence-human was safe, Zamboni refocused his attention on his mortal enemies—the chipmunks. They were abundant among the town, even more so than the squirrels. But the chipmunks were crafty, with their intricate underground burrows connecting through the neighborhood. Zamboni had nearly caught one several times, only for it to scamper into a nearby hole.

He dragged his nose along the ground, searching for any trace of a fresh scent. After he'd circled the yard twice, he huffed in disappointment. The chipmunks had gotten smarter, avoiding Zamboni's yard entirely. His ears perked up when the sliding door opened and his owner, Krystal, popped her head out. He rocketed over to her, tail wagging with abandon. She smiled and sunk her fingers into his thick fur, scratching the sensitive spot behind his ears. His tongue lolled from his mouth in ecstasy.

"Zambo! How's my good boy? Want to go for a walk?"

Zamboni barked and ran in a small circle while Krystal retrieved the leash from a hook on the wall. She snapped it on his collar and jogged with him to the front door. After locking the door, the pair bounded down the sidewalk. True to his Siberian Husky breed, Zamboni had only two speeds: trot and sprint. Krystal usually had to jog to keep his pace, but if he felt the leash going taut, he would slow his gait just enough for her to catch up.

They passed other townspeople on their morning romp who all waved and said, "Good morning". Many greeted Zamboni with shouts of his name. He'd always perk his ears in the direction of the sound, but until Krystal and he reached the town hall, he would not stop. The two ran past a series of well-manicured homes. The humans seemed to think this was a beautiful spot for pictures, but Zamboni didn't understand what was so exciting about the gray homes. Finally, they reached the building, nestled atop the one hill in town. An expansive garden full of flowery scents unfurled itself before them as they crested the top.

Zamboni inhaled deeply. Beneath the aromatic smells of the daisies and roses, he could scent chipmunk. It was no secret that the rodents made their nest beneath the town square garden. The humans had once attempted to remove the pests, but once the rodents were classified endangered, the good humans of Wellsprings adapted, co-existing with the beasts. It was even said that the town had the highest number of Palmer chipmunks in the entire country.

Krystal panted and leaned against a vending machine on the side of the town hall. This was where the community bulletin area was. Posters of male humans were plastered to the bricks of the wall beside the community board. Zamboni pulled on the lead and Krystal released him, as was their usual practice. Krystal's attention strayed to a paper on the community board as Zamboni thundered about the garden. He would normally duck behind the building where there were strings of large bushes. Zamboni followed his own scent to the area off to the right. He found his hole there and he got to work pulling up dirt by the mounds.

Zamboni had to make quick work of his digging. The chipmunk den was directly below him and the rodents had just started to slip into hibernation. Normally, they would be totally defenseless in the winter months, but the wily creatures would stir every few days to drowsily munch on stolen food and raise their body temperatures before falling asleep for another few days. They would certainly wake in the coming hours, but for now, Zamboni couldn't hear movement.

"Zamboni! Come here, boy," Krystal hollered. Zamboni popped his head out of the pit. Krystal was calling him back early. Zamboni quickly scrambled to get a few more paws full of soil before climbing out. He shook the dirt off and bounded off toward his owner. She was holding a paper, assumingly ripped from the bulletin board. Her eyes glittered when they caught sight of Zamboni. She showed him the paper, a wide smile on her face. Zamboni tilted his head. Surely, she knew he didn't know what the paper was.

"Hey Zambo, want to do something crazy?"

# Chapter 5

## Sebastian

Why hadn't he left his number?

It had been nearly a week, and he couldn't stop thinking about his encounter with Cruella in the bar. He'd never shared a kiss with anyone nearly as intense. Sebastian knew if he hadn't been surrounded by the other bar patrons, he'd have gone much further. He grunted and scrubbed a hand down his face before returning to the muffin batter he'd been beating into submission. When Sebastian was stressed, he baked. He should really put the spatula down. He needed to focus on the upcoming holiday festival—he and his campaign team would be operating a booth alongside Clay Emerson and company.

Wellsprings had a funny way of prioritizing the Christmas season over any other event... like perhaps the impending mayoral election at the end of March. No doubt, he and Clay would be subject to countless holiday themed appearances. Sebastian ground his teeth. If they even *thought* about dressing him in a Santa suit, he'd gladly set the town ablaze.

Sebastian poured the batter into his lined muffin tray and slid it into the oven. Tossing his oven mitts aside, he hopped onto a kitchen stool and studied the booth layout again. If there weren't any last-minute changes, the elusive Stella Simmons would be in the booth across from theirs. Hopefully, he'll be able to get a few words in to pitch his—or Victor's—idea. Sebastian jotted some notes before his cell started buzzing in a frenzy. He sighed, stood from his stool, and took the call out on the balcony. He hadn't had a chance to say hello before his father barked at him.

"What the *hell* did you do?"

"Dad, specifics. What are you accusing me of now?"

"Check the town paper," Victor ground out before hanging up. Sebastian's pulse raced. He nabbed his keys from the counter and jogged out the front door, only a smidge worried about leaving the oven unattended. He attempted to get his pounding heart under control. *It can't be that bad. Right?*

A small publication rack was at the front of his apartment building, a plastic yellow beacon of doom. Sebastian deposited a quarter and retrieved his copy. The headline read: Candidate Rivera Consorting with de Vil? And below the bold letters was him. In his phoenix mask. Kissing the ever-loving-fuck out of Cruella de Vil.

"Jesus H. Christ," he whispered under his breath. He took the offending paper with him back to his apartment, spreading it out on the kitchen island. He skimmed the article to see if they mentioned the bar was LGBTQ. They said the name but, thankfully, that was all. The picture itself was grainy at best. There was no way to tell it was Sebastian under the mask unless someone had seen him prior to the bar. He scrutinized Cruella. There was no possible means to prove he was a man. His drag was decent, fake tits and all. He exhaled a long breath before calling his father back.

"You saw?"

"Yes, I saw. I wouldn't worry. No one can tell it was me. I was wearing a mask." Sebastian forced a smile on his face as the next words tumbled out of him like poison sludge. "And who cares if I was kissing some random chick at a bar?"

"People are talking. I know what kind of place that is." Sebastian's stomach sank. The Riveras had always quietly danced around the subject of Sebastian's sexual preference. He hadn't tried to hide it from them, but stubborn as ever, they pretended they didn't know. His father strongly disapproved without ever actually saying he did. Sebastian had a feeling that if the town discovered he was homosexual that his father would make him pay… most likely by revoking inheritance and cash flow from the family funds.

"It was the least crowded bar I could find." Truth. "Plenty of straight people go to gay bars, you know." Truth. "And besides, it was a girl I kissed." Lie. Lie. Lie. Lie.

"Hmm. Well, if that's the case, what was her name?"

"Her name?" He looked back down at the photo. "Ella. Why?"

"Ella, huh? Well, why don't you bring her to Sunday dinner?"

"Wait, you want me to invite a woman I barely know to a family dinner? Are you crazy? I don't even have her contact info."

"Fine. One month. Find her, woo her. Make this real so that you don't make your family look like a joke."

"A month?!" Sebastian sputtered and pinched the bridge of his nose in frustration. "Dad, is this more important than the election? Because I distinctly remember you telling me that if I lost, you'd disown me."

"You are my son and capable of juggling more than one task. One month," Victor said before disconnecting. Sebastian growled in frustration and threw the phone across the room. It skittered along the tile floor and landed on his area rug. Sebastian cursed and plucked the phone from the floor. It now had several cracks in the screen, even underneath the shattered glass screen protector. It was still functional thanks to his military grade case.

He cursed again and looked up the number to the bar. He dialed the number and paced around the brown leather couch in his living room. A tired woman's voice answered.

"Hideyhole. This is Roxy," she huffed into the phone. There was a din of noise in the background—glasses clinking and running water predominantly.

"Hi Roxy. Do you happen to know who was bartending on Halloween night?"

"That was me. What can I do for you?"

"Oh, um. Do you remember a man dressed in a phoenix mask that gave you a hundred-dollar tip? That was me." He rolled his eyes at his own words. He was sure he sounded like a pompous ass.

"Oh, yes! That was exceedingly generous of you. Thank you." He could hear the hesitation in her voice.

"Oh, it was no problem." He facepalmed. "I mean… do you know the person I was talking to at the bar? They were dressed as Cruella? I lost their number that night and I really wanted to reach out."

"Well… I'm not exactly at liberty to discuss my patrons," she said with steel in her voice.

He sighed deeply and tried his last tactic. Tug the heartstrings.

"Dammit. I think he was the love of my life. God, I fucked up." He let emotion leak into his voice, banging his fist against the coffee table for emphasis. "Well, thank you for your time–"

"Wait!"

Sebastian fist pumped the air and put hope in his voice. "Yes?!"

"You're not a stalker or anything? I can give you a phone number. Whether or not they answer you is up to them. But if you get weird, I won't hesitate to file harassment charges."

"Thank you so much, Roxy. I promise I'm not a creeper."

"Yeah, yeah... you got a pen, birdman?"

# CHAPTER 6

## Clay

C lay groaned, massaging his temples. He had his sunglasses firmly in place, sitting at his sister's kitchen table. His niece was sitting beside him, chattering away about the unicorn she was drawing.

"Unkie Clay, unicorns only have one horn. Not two," Clarissa gar-
bled. All of her L's and R's sounded like W's, so she called him *Unkie
Cway*. Which was so fucking cute Clay might have punched himself in
the face if he wasn't so hungover. She tapped her pink crayon against
his forearm when he didn't answer right away.

"Yes, Clarissa, you're absolutely right," he winced at hearing his
own voice. Cameron raised her eyebrow at him as she slid over a
Bloody Mary, her soft brown eyes rolling.

"Who gets piss drunk on a Wednesday night? You're insane. I can't
drink like that without being dead for days."

Clay pointedly looked down at her pregnant belly.

"Well, I'd venture to say you haven't drunk in about seven months."
Clay pulled up his sunglasses to narrow his eyes at her.

"Shut up butt plug, you know what I mean." She threw a dish towel at him, and he snorted a laugh.

"Mommy, what's a butt plug?" Clarissa blinked her big blue eyes at Cameron. Clay guffawed into his drink. The tangy and spicy combination cleared his head.

"Um... something icky, honey. Why don't you go wake up Charlie? Tell him breakfast is almost ready."

"Okaaaaaay!" Clarissa hopped out of her chair and zoomed away with airplane arms. Clay glanced over at Clarissa's drawing. It looked suspiciously phallic. Clay's phone chimed in rapid fire and he groaned, taking a long sip of his Bloody Mary.

"Someone's popular. Shouldn't you answer that? It could be related to the campaign," Cameron said in between flipping pancakes. Her husband, Colby, popped his head in the kitchen, said his hellos, kissed his wife on her head, and took the spatula from her, ushering her to sit beside Clay.

"Clay, make sure she doesn't get up. She needs to focus on growing our baby," Colby chastised before returning to the pancakes. Clay's phone went off again, making Cameron flare her nostrils at him. She notoriously hated it when people ignored their messages.

"It's not about the campaign. I met a guy last night and he won't stop texting me." Clay propped his glasses on top of his head to roll his eyes at her. Clay's nephew chose that moment to sleepily drag himself into the kitchen.

"Mom, why is Clarissa calling me a butt plug?" He slipped his gangly teenage body into the open seat at Clay's right and Cameron slapped her palm against her forehead, cursing quietly under her breath. "You met someone, Uncle Clay?"

"Eh... kinda? Not really..." Clay wasn't sure how to frame his response with his sister and brother-in-law in earshot. If they were alone, the two would gush over him.

"Oh, so you just hooked up, then?" Charlie sipped on some orange juice from the pitcher while his mom scolded him.

"I suppose you can say that. How are things going at school? Meet any cute people?" Charlie looked away, picking non-existent lint off his shirt.

"Nah. Things are fine," he mumbled.

"Did you try out for *Dear Evan Hansen*? I remember you saying the tryouts were coming up." Clay sucked down his drink, making suction noises with the straw.

"Oh. They haven't happened yet." Charlie kept his eyes down. Clay looked over at Cameron, who had her mouth in a tense line. They knew Charlie was being bullied at school. They weren't sure yet if it was because he'd come out as bisexual. But Clay grew up in Wellsprings. He went to Wellsprings High. He knew how the kids around here could be. That was why Clay was so intent on getting an anti-bullying program going.

"Charlie, why don't you go get dressed while Dad finishes breakfast?" Cameron smiled at her son. He nodded and excused himself from the table.

"So, they're still bothering him?" Clay frowned at his sister.

"I assume so. He doesn't talk to me. I was hoping you might walk him to school and have a chat with him?"

"Ah, so that's why you invited me for breakfast. But you don't have to bribe me with food for me to spend time with my darling nephew." Clay's phone pinged again, and he groaned when Cameron looked at him sharply. "Fine!"

He flipped his phone over on the table to see four texts.

Unknown

Hey. This is the guy from Halloween.

The phoenix.

I got your number from Roxy. Don't freak out.

Think we could meet for coffee? I'll be at Jenny's Cafe in Wellsprings at 9 today. Please. It's important.

"Holy shit! Holy shit! Holy shit! It's the guy from Halloween! The Phoenix!" Clay's heart pounded loudly as he showed his sister the texts. She gasped and grabbed his hands.

"Clay! You have to go! You can walk Charlie to school another day. Go get your man!" The two of them squealed like schoolgirls for a moment before Clay jumped to his feet and fired off a response.

I'll be there.

Clay ran his fingers through his hair, acutely aware of how disheveled he looked in his Penn State hoodie and gray sweats. He'd planned on changing before heading to the campaign offices. But he figured he could play it off as if he'd just finished a run. Clay sucked in a deep breath and lightly jogged the five minutes to Jenny's. By the time he arrived, he was winded and dripping in sweat. He took a moment to catch his breath and check to see the time. He was fifteen minutes early. Might as well get a coffee and pick up a paper while he was there.

The door jangled happily as he entered the quaint coffee shop with a used bookstore attached. Since Starbucks had moved into Wellsprings, Jenny's had been struggling to compete. On principle, Clay was sure to always purchase his caffeine here, supporting the local business. Unlike the Rivera family. If it hadn't been for Victor Rivera, Wellsprings wouldn't have as many big box stores and the mom-and-pop shops could have stayed afloat. Sadly, many businesses had shut their doors in the past years.

Clay greeted Jenny at the counter, ordered his usual latte and picked up the paper. He paid, tipping generously, and took office in the corner booth. He spied Sebastian Rivera in a booth directly in his eyesight. His hulking frame was hunched over an espresso cup, glaring down at his phone.

Clay rolled his eyes, sipped his latte, and glanced down at the paper. He read the headline, saw the picture, and choked on his coffee. He coughed loudly, inviting the unwanted gaze of Sebastian who scowled and looked away quickly.

Clay blinked rapidly, desperately trying to get his brain to reconnect to the brainstem. *No way. It can't be.* He yanked his phone from his pocket and texted the Phoenix.

> I'm here.

His eyes whipped up to watch Sebastian with bated breath. *See? I knew it wasn't him.* Sebastian's phone chimed deafeningly, and he scrambled to read the incoming message. Sebastian's honey brown eyes looked up in panic and watched the door. When no one entered, he stood from his booth and scanned the cafe. They traveled over the mother and her toddler, an older gentleman, and then fell on Clay.

Sebastian froze, all the color draining from his face. Clay stared him down, paper still clutched in his left hand, phone in his right. Sebastian's jaw stiffened, and he picked up his tiny espresso cup, making his way to Clay's booth. They regarded each other wordlessly for a moment before speaking.

"Cruella?" Sebastian's Adam's apple bobbed.

"Phoenix?" Clay's voice wavered and Sebastian's shoulders fell.

"Fuck," he grumbled, rubbing his palm down his face and fell into the booth. Sebastian dug his fingers into his hair and stared down at the Formica table.

"You're gay?" Clay blurted nervously, immediately taking a long hot sip of his drink to shut his dumb ass up. Sebastian glanced at him and rolled his eyes, releasing the hold on his hair.

"Clearly, Mr. Emerson." His face was tight. Probably as tight as his ass.

"Oh, please. I think we're past formalities, Sebastian. Well... you said it was urgent."

"Ah, yes... about that... Clay," he said his name as if he was trying to see how it tasted in his mouth. "I have a bit of a problem. See... my parents are either extremely homophobic or insanely ignorant. They think I was kissing a woman that night. And well... they want to meet her... er, you. And I have a suspicious feeling that if I don't introduce you to them, I may be disinherited." Sebastian winced and rubbed the back of his neck nervously. Clay was trying to ignore how cute that was and instead focused on the big wrench in this plan.

"Um... Sebastian. One tiny problem. Not sure if you've noticed... I'm a man," Clay twirled his coffee cup, feet securely on the ground, trying to remind himself that this was, in fact, really happening. Sebastian glared at him.

"I'm acutely aware of that. Not to mention we're rivals... God, I know this is going to sound ridiculous and wildly insensitive... but your drag was pretty spot on." He looked at Clay, hopeful that he'd fill in the blanks on his own. It was Clay's turn to glare.

"You want me to dress in drag and pretend to be your girlfriend?"

"Basically, yes." Clay stared at him incredulously. Sure, he dressed in drag for fun sometimes, but he was in no way a professional queen. But maybe he could get something for his trouble.

"Say I agree. What would I get out of this little deal?"

"If I win the election... I'll take up your anti-bullying agenda."

Clay's sassy attitude quickly disappeared. Storm clouds quickly formed in his mossy green eyes. He could feel the rage building in his chest. Unbidden flashes rushed back to him. Tears. Blood. Bruises. The creaking of a rope. Clay stood abruptly, a fire in his eyes.

"How *dare* you? You have no right. Not when you and your buddies tortured Tobias and I for every fucking year of high school! Not after—"

"Hey! I had nothing to do with that shit. It was all Jesse. He was a piece of crap."

"But you sat there, and you *watched*. You did nothing to stop it! And you're gay on top of it?! I can't even look at you, you fucking coward." Clay rushed for the exit, sure that Jenny overheard Clay's outburst. He threw an apologetic smile at her before throwing the door open. He could hear the thundering steps of Sebastian behind him.

"Clay, wait!"

Clay turned to face him, fury etched on his face. Sebastian glanced around him and grabbed Clay by the elbow, dragging him across the street to the empty park.

"Clay, you're right. But I was afraid. I was still in the closet. I never took part in anything that went down there. And Tobias... what happened was tragic and so wrong..." Sebastian trailed off when Clay's tears bubbled down his cheeks. He couldn't stop the sob crawling from his chest. Clay hid his face in his hands as sobs racked through his body. A large, warm hand slid up and down his back, a hard wall of muscle against his cheek. Sebastian Rivera was hugging him, and he smelled *good*. He smelled of musk and vanilla, and fucking delicious.

"I'm so sorry, Clay. I'm so, so sorry," he grumbled emotionally. The big bear of a man softened a bit. They stood there in an awkward embrace until Clay pulled away with an unnerving amount of difficulty, silently turning to walk down the sidewalk. He may have glanced over his shoulder to see the big hulk of a man plopped on a bench, hands in his hair, shoulders trembling. *Don't go back, Clay. Let him sit with it.* Clay absently rubbed at his forearms and his scars, unable to erase the chill that settled there.

# Chapter 7

## Sebastian

He was wearing a goddamn Santa suit. Sebastian scowled behind his synthetic white beard as children lined up to sit on his lap. He locked eyes with Marc, who was standing to the left of the growing crowd. He fought back a smile and Sebastian rolled his eyes at him.

"Of course they made the gay guy the elf," an irritated voice mumbled behind him. Another voice whispered with him.

"It's not because you're gay, Clay. I think you'd be more offended if they asked you to be Mrs. Claus." Sebastian recognized the voice as Jade, Clay's guard.

"Well, yes... but I could totally rock that costume. Why does *he* get to be Santa? He's a huge jerk."

"Could you imagine that guy as an elf? I'd shit my pants if I was one of those kids having Elf Sebastian towering over me." Jade snorted a laugh, and Clay sighed.

"I guess you're right. Hope you're free tonight. I'm going to need a drink after this."

"I will clear my schedule. Now get out there, Jingles."

Clay scoffed at Jade and suddenly appeared by Sebastian's side. He could tell Clay was leaning away from him as much as the space allowed. They hadn't spoken since their fight in the park, which meant Sebastian had made no progress with him. The clock was ticking.

"Do you think they hate us?" Sebastian asked, hoping he sounded lighthearted. Clay's eyes swiveled to him, venom still lurking in his emerald gaze. "The council?"

"Hm. I'd say this is a trial. To see how we act with the residents." Clay forced his eyes away, smiling brightly at the children at the gate. Said council members were milling about the hot chocolate booth directly beside them. Their eyes were all aimed in their direction.

"Clay, could we go somewhere after this? Discuss... things?"

"Sorry Santa, I have plans tonight." Clay met his eyes again, calculating his next words. "Ask me tomorrow."

Clay swiftly moved to let the first child in, giving Sebastian a wonderful view of his ass in the skintight elf pants. *Damn.*

The hour trudged past as Sebastian slowly melted to death in his Santa suit. He was more than a little irritated when a stubborn kid complained about not getting the puppy he'd asked for last Christmas. Sebastian sighed heavily and tried his best not to scream at the kid.

"Well, a pet is a big commitment. Sometimes we want things, but it isn't the right time. If you keep being a good boy, you may get exactly what you want."

"But I want a puppy!" The boy screamed and kicked Sebastian directly in the shin before hopping off his lap and running back to his horrified parents. They mouthed their apology before ushering the demon spawn away.

Sebastian cursed quietly and rubbed his shin before Clay stepped up to the gate and called to the remaining children in line.

"Okay, everyone, Santa needs a quick cookie break. We'll be back in thirty minutes!" A few kids squealed as their parents pulled them from the line to occupy them elsewhere. Clay turned to Sebastion.

"Thank you," Sebastian said, rising to his feet. He rolled his shoulders to unwind his stiff muscles.

"Yeah, well, I need to get out of this outfit. I'm dying." Clay moved past him and ducked into the gym behind them. The owner had agreed to offer their locker room and showers during the holiday festival. Sebastian followed, thinking of different ways to broach the whole dinner subject. He pulled off his beard and was unbuttoning the Santa jacket when he entered the locker room, where he was greeted by Clay's perky bare ass.

Sebastian could feel his cheeks heating as several pornographic scenarios traipsed through his mind. He shook his head and turned his back, offering privacy. The sound of a shower signaled Clay had left. Sebastian quickly stripped out of the sweat soaked costume and turned to grab his own shower, only to come face to face with Clay.

Clay's brilliant green eyes bulged as he took in Sebastion's semi-erect cock. His eyes traveled up, ogling Sebastian's muscular chest before remembering to cover himself. Sebastian had already taken his own examination. Clay was thin with lean muscles. His pale skin was dusted with freckles and lightly coated with red chest hair that matched the hair on his head… and pubic region. Sebastian's eyes drifted to his forearms where the light pink scar tissue glared at him.

"Forgot my towel," Clay mumbled before rushing back to the showers, flashing his naked ass again. Sebastian blinked slowly, looking down at his now fully erect self. He sighed, gripped his length forlornly, and moved into the shower beside Clay.

Sebastian stood under the warm spray for a while before hearing a soft moan from the shower stall beside him. His heart stopped as he strained to listen. Sure enough, another quiet groan traveled through the water spray. Sebastian's dick twitched, still painfully erect. He bit his lip and gripped himself tightly. Another breathy noise sounded, and Sebastian pumped himself, making his own grunt of pleasure.

The noises went silent for a moment before starting back up, less quiet than before. Sebastian braced an arm against the wall of the shower and pumped himself with abandon, letting his own noises mingle in the steamy air. He rotated the previous dirty thoughts in his head before a sharp inhale came from his neighbor, followed by a long, muffled moan. Sebastian's peak crested after that and he came, almost violently, on the shower floor.

The two were silent, the gravity of what had just happened slowly sinking in. Clay's shower turned off first and Sebastian waited for him to pass, giving him privacy. Once he'd figured enough time had elapsed, he killed the water, stepping out naked and dripping wet. He hadn't grabbed a towel either. He shuffled into the locker room and found Clay clad in boxer-briefs, sitting on a bench, most likely having an existential crisis judging by the way he wrung his hands.

His green eyes looked up at Sebastian, pointedly ignoring his nakedness. When he said nothing, Sebastian huffed and strode past him. No sense in feigning modesty now. They'd already seen each other naked. He pulled a folded towel from a shelf and roughly dried his hair before slinging it around his waist. Clay was suddenly at his side, clearing his throat.

Sebastian looked down at him, hoping he gave off an indifferent air, because in reality, he was freaking out on the inside. *Holy shit, holy shit, holy shit! That just happened. Be cool, Sebastian. Don't freak him out.* His pulse was still thundering in his chest. He'd been intimate with men before, but he hadn't allowed himself to have many encounters. *Because you don't deserve it.* His mind was always sure to remind him of that. That's why he'd left on Halloween.

"So," Clay hedged, "maybe we should get that drink then?"

# Chapter 8

## Clay

Watching Sebastian Rivera attempt to be a jolly fat man was the highlight of Clay's week. It was painfully obvious how uncomfortable he was with children. Especially when they cried. He was awkwardly holding a screaming baby while the mother attempted acrobatics to get a decent photo.

"My god, you're hopeless," Clay muttered under his breath, just loud enough for Sebastian to hear. He moved over to them in his jingling elf costume.

"Hi there, sweetie! It's okay, there's nothing to be afraid of. Mommy is right here," Clay said, angling the mom to be in the baby's line of sight better and asked the photographer to move in at a different angle. "Okay, now Santa, look down at the baby." Sebastian did as he was instructed, and the baby calmed enough to salvage the photo shoot. The mother thanked Clay with a big hug and scooped up her fussy little girl.

"Wow, you're really good with kids," Sebastian said, muffled by his synthetic beard. Clay propped his hip against Santa's chair while they enjoyed a brief lull in kids.

"Yeah, I'm a Guncle. Had a bit of practice." Clay accepted a bottle of water from one of his booth-mates and took a long swig before looking down at Sebastian as he struggled to drink from his own water bottle with his beard on. "I take it you don't want any kids." He wouldn't be shocked. Sebastian was too rich and too selfish.

"Well... it's complicated, as I'm sure you're aware." He shifted the bottle in thought. "I've actually always wanted a big family." *Huh.* "But I'm realistic. I know there are limitations. It's not that I don't like kids, they just make me nervous."

The pair looked out at the dwindling crowd solemnly. Kids were a heavy topic for a gay man. *Smooth move, Clay.*

"I want kids, too," he said softly before a few more children lined up for Santa.

Twenty minutes later, they were wrapping up the booth. Clay stretched and made a note to soak his feet. They had to do this for the rest of the week.

Clay made sure he didn't follow Sebastian into the gym this time. He wasn't sure he could trust his libido to stay in check if he caught another glimpse of that man's body. He was drinking water when the realization came crashing into him. *Holy fuck, we masturbated in tandem with each other's sex sounds. What the actual fuck?*

He choked on his water, drawing Jade's attention. He waved her off, but she had a huge grin on her face, which usually meant trouble.

"So, are we on tonight for drinks?"

"Oh, shit. Sorry, Jade. I forgot I suggested that... could we reschedule? This whole elf costume thing has made me want to burn my skin off. I really need to soak in the tub for five hours."

"No worries... I was kind of going to blow you off, anyway." She looked meaningfully over her shoulder at Marc, Sebastian's security detail. Bless him, he was trying to appear official and scanning the area, but his eyes kept catching on Jade. Marc was another of Sebastian's friends in high school. Though he had nothing to do with the bullying. He was more of a gentle giant. Clay approved.

"Get yo' man, girl. You'd better climb him like a tree. I expect a full report tomorrow."

"Sir, yes, sir!" She saluted and gave him a little half-hug before waltzing over to a grinning Marc. Clay smiled at the lovebirds and finally made his way into the gym. Sebastian was dressed back in the blue plaid button up and faded blue jeans he'd arrived in, hair freshly showered. Clay moved past him, remembering to grab a towel for his quick (chaste) shower.

He was clean in minutes, clad in a towel, holding his sweaty elf costume. Sebastian waited outside the door to the locker room. Clay was grateful he'd had enough foresight to wear a salmon button up and beige khakis. He unbuttoned the first two buttons and rolled the cuffs for a more casual look and donned his black faux leather jacket.

Sebastian was puffing on an e-cigarette when Clay joined him. Clay grimaced at the e-cigarette involuntarily. *Ew.* Sebastian raised an eyebrow and stuffed the offending device away.

"So, do you know any nice unassuming bars outside of town? I can't show my face at The Hideyhole for a while." Sebastian wormed his hands into his peacoat pockets, clearly trying to look more at ease than he must be feeling.

"Yeah sure. I'll drive."

Twenty minutes and one painfully awkward car ride later, they took a seat in the corner of McFaddin's, a quiet Irish pub just outside of Wellsprings. Sebastian's head was constantly swiveling, probably making sure nobody he knew could see them conspiring together. Clay ordered a dirty martini and a side of nachos.

"Okay. You have until I finish my drink and chips. Go."

"Wh—" Sebastian cleared his voice. "Well, as I'd explained at the cafe, I sort of need 'Ella' to come to Sunday dinner with me three weeks from now and pretend to be my girlfriend."

"To clarify," Clay paused to accept the martini from the waiter, "you want *me* to dress in drag and pretend to be your girlfriend to secure your future inheritance? *Me*, your political rival."

"Look, I know it sounds stupid. But you're the only one who knows about me. It would be too difficult and counterintuitive to bring someone else in on the plan." Sebastian signaled the waiter again and ordered a whisky, neat.

"And our deal? If you win the candidacy, you'll take over the anti-bullying program... but what if I win? Then this deal is moot, is it not?" Clay took a long satisfying sip of his martini while Sebastian stressfully ran fingers through his hair.

"Then let's sweeten the pot. Regardless of who wins, I'll personally fund the program, using money from my trust fund. So long as my parents don't cut me off, that is." Sebastian leveled a sturdy look at him. Clay's jaw hung open slightly. Not needing to allocate funds to the anti-bullying program would free up money that could be used in the school. It was really a no-brainer. "However," Clay immediately scowled at him, "I have a caveat. I want our act to be convincing. Leave no room for doubt. So that means we need to practice."

"Practice what, exactly?"

"Dates. We need to go on practice dates. Get to know each other well enough to make a month-long relationship plausible. That shouldn't be too difficult."

"I assume you'd want me in drag for these dates? To be in public?"

"Yes… so are you in?" The waiter returned with Sebastian's drink and nachos. Sebastian took a long swallow of his whisky and waited for Clay's answer.

"Okay, Sebastian. I'm in." Clay held out his hand and Sebastian smiled lopsidedly, shaking his hand.

"About that, you should call me Bas from now on. Only my father calls me by my full name."

"Noted. So how many times should we meet?"

"How do Tuesdays and Thursdays for the next three weeks sound?"

"Doable." In the sports bar, a group of men howled in excitement at whatever touchdown happened on TV.

"Hm… I miss football," Sebastian said softly, eyes following Clay's. He spun his highball glass before taking another sip of whisky.

"Oh, that's right. You played in high school. What position were you? I was never into sports, so I made a conscious effort to ignore it."

Sebastian snorted a laugh and stole a chip from Clay's basket. "I was running back. I liked how simple it was. Get the ball. Run."

"Gee, it must have been nice hanging around all those tight ends," Clay sighed wistfully, propping his chin on his palm. "Besides all the homophobic behavior, of course." Clay laughed dryly and absently dug around the chip basket. "And to think I had a big crush on you back then. How funny."

Sebastian choked on his whisky. "Crush?"

"Oh, sure. I mean, you were hot. Had a great body… I mean, you still do." Clay's eyes slowly rose to meet Sebastian's. "Okay, I'm making this weird." His cheeks flushed, and he threw back the rest of his martini to deflect. "So, what about you? Who were you crushing on in High School?"

Sebastian's shoulders stiffened. He propped his elbows on the table, threaded his fingers together, and brought them in front of his lips. He stared at Clay, not speaking. Clay raised an eyebrow and folded his arms on the table.

"Why are you staring like that—wait. No," Clay's eyes widened in shock and the corner of a smirk peeked out behind Sebastian's hands. "No way. *Me*? How?!"

"What can I say? I have a thing for redheads." Sebastian grinned slyly.

"How could we both have had crushes on each other? And nothing happened?"

"Well, you ended up with Tobias."

The air turned stale between them at the mention of Tobias. Clay felt like a bucket of ice water had been splashed on his face. *How dare you flirt with this asshole? Remember what he did...? Or rather, didn't do.*

"Well, I'm afraid I have to get going." Clay quickly scooted out of the booth.

"Wait, Clay!"

Clay shot him a withering look over his shoulder. Sebastian had been reaching out a hand to stop him, but quickly snatched it back.

"I'll text you next date's details?"

"Sure. See ya, Bas." Clay turned on his heel and didn't look back.

# CHAPTER 9

## Sebastian

Sebastian's heart bumped hard against his rib cage when Clay called him Bas. He slumped against the back of his seat, chewing his lip in thought. He helped himself to the remaining nachos and pulled out his phone, figuring he should save Clay's number now. First, he typed in "Clay Emerson" but quickly deleted it in case someone saw him texting his political rival. He typed "Ella," paused, then deleted it again. He settled on "Redhead from the bar" instead. Less incriminating.

He quickly pulled up a search engine to look up what events were being held around the town that could be good date spots. Of course, the good ol' town hall had a list of upcoming events. He took a screenshot and checked his schedule. Thankfully, they could make most of the events. Being at crowded town events would probably be in the plan's best interest. Sure, that was totally the only reason.

Sebastian paid the bill and headed out into the chilly night air. Luckily, his apartment was only a few blocks away, so he headed in that direction. He fired off a text to Clay once he'd reached his building's doors.

> The Christmas charity hockey game is in two days. There will be a ton of eyes there. Maybe a good day for our debut?

Redhead from the bar

> What is it with this town and Christmas?

> Sounds good tho. Anything specific you want me to wear?

Sebastian hesitated at the elevator, a slew of inappropriate replies coming to mind. He went the safe route.

> It's an ice rink, not a runway. Dress warmly.

God, he sounded like a grumpy old dad. He got to his apartment and chucked his duffle with the soiled Santa suit into the laundry room. He was pulling his sneakers off when his phone chirped again.

> Yes, Daddy.

The text was followed by a picture of Clay, shirtless, and in a red wig, blowing a kiss to the camera.

> Red wig, huh?

> I can't let a redhead fan down, now, can I?

Sebastian grinned and was about to text back when his phone rang. His dad never called him later than eight thirty. It must be important.

"Hey, Dad?"

"How did it go with Miss Simmons today?" No greeting, per usual.

"I was very busy today." Busy jerking off in the shower with Clay. "I intend to speak with her tomorrow," he said gruffly.

"You'd better. But that's not the only reason for my call." Victor's tone changed to a more solemn one. Sebastian was immediately on the defensive.

"Is something wrong?"

"In a sense. Another mayoral candidate was just announced."

# CHAPTER 10

## Clay

"A dog?" Clay asked Tanya, his lead campaign manager. Tanya nodded, handing Clay a clipboard with several articles and the newest candidate's photo. A doofy-looking Siberian Husky grinned back at him with ice-blue eyes.

"This could be a serious threat to our camp and Rivera's. Small towns go apeshit for animal mayors," Tanya sighed, making herself at home in his green velvet armchair. She'd caught him watering his plants in his underwear when she'd burst in that morning, having used her emergency key. He'd located a robe while she prattled on about a "catastrophic problem."

"I fail to see why this warranted an early morning house raid, Tanya." He handed the clipboard back to her and watered his finicky fiddle leaf fig.

"Zamboni is going to stop by the booth today. He'll take a shift as Santa Paws, which gives you and Rivera a longer break."

Clay rolled his eyes skyward. "My god, what even is this conversation?"

"This is serious, Clay. You'll need to hold an additional rally or something. I'm sure the Rivera camp is discussing their own strategies."

Clay groaned and stepped into his bedroom to dress while Tanya yelled workable ideas through the closed door. He knew he should focus on the campaign and put more effort into listening to Tanya's advice. But his head was filled with ideas for the anti-bullying program Sebastian Rivera would be funding.

He exited his room, fully dressed, and shot Tanya a withering look. She sat ramrod straight, poised, awaiting instruction.

"Let's schedule it for after Thanksgiving," Tanya started jotting notes. "Since this town loves Christmas so much, why don't we make it like a carol sing-a-long?"

"Oh, great idea. They'll eat that shit up."

Clay pulled his elf costume from the dryer and stuffed it into a canvas bag. Tanya yanked his coat from the hanger and tossed it at him, simultaneously opening the door. He chuckled to himself and shook his head. He'd hired Tanya because of her tenacity. If anyone could plan a successful campaign against a pupper, it was her.

The two quickly made their way downtown. They were late to the booth, though. The Rivera camp had already begun setting up. Someone handed Clay a hot cocoa and the space quickly erupted into the chaos of setup. The air had a bit more of a bite to it that morning, and Clay was happy to have the warmth of sweet chocolate gold between his palms. He said his good mornings and headed into the gym to change into his elf costume while his team hustled about.

Sebastian was nearly finished getting dressed in his Santa suit, red pants slung low on his hips, jacket unbuttoned showing his bare chest. *Ho ho ho, Daddy.*

"Hey," Sebastian said in a gruff voice. He was totally *not* a morning person.

"Hey, Bas."

Sebastian paused, his fingers hovering over the first jacket button. His face was unreadable, and he quickly made work of the buttons. Clay shook his head and started changing out of his clothes. When he stepped into the one-piece elf costume, he froze. Something seemed off about the costume.

He pulled it up to his hips and looked down in horror. The costume must have shrunk in the wash and was now clinging to Clay's junk and ass like its life depended on it. The legs even came up midway on his calf. He swallowed a lump in his throat and struggled to pull the costume the rest of the way on. It was like a body glove, arms too short, neckline low. He could barely move.

"Well, shit," Clay said to no one in particular.

"Problem?" Sebastian grumbled behind him. Clay winced and turned to show him. Sebastian's eyes almost popped out of his skull, zeroing in on Clay's pelvic area.

"Must have shrunk in the wash," Clay laughed nervously, turning to face the lockers. He heard Sebastian inhale sharply and a rustling of fabric behind him. Warm fabric suddenly engulfed his shoulders. It smelled of musky cologne with a hint of something sweet. Clay knew he was blushing, but he looked up at Sebastian's equally flushed face. He'd given him the Santa jacket, his chest now bare. "Thanks, Bas."

Sebastian swallowed loudly and said he'd be right back. Clay smiled stupidly and snuggled into the coat. "Mmm... damn, he smells good."

"Ahem," Tanya said, suddenly appearing at his elbow. He yelped in surprise.

"Jesus, you're like a ninja!"

"Mr. Rivera said you needed help?" Tanya adjusted her glasses and peered down at the costume. Clay opened the coat to give her a better view. "Yikes! I don't need to see that, Clay. I'll have the party store deliver a replacement." Tanya was on her phone a heartbeat later, yelling demands at some poor underpaid employee. Sebastian hovered by the door. Still clad in his Santa pants and bare chest.

"You should probably take this back. You have no shirt." Clay shrugged out of the coat, only to meet a scowling Sebastian.

"I gave it to you. Keep it. I don't want it." He pushed off the wall he'd been lounging on and made his way over to Clay's bench. They sat at opposite ends, waiting for the costume to be delivered. "Oh, while we're alone." Sebastian hopped up and ransacked his duffle. He returned to his seat, holding out a paper to Clay. "Your ticket for the hockey game."

"Oh, thanks." Clay stowed the ticket in his bag just as a harried young man burst through the gym doors. He was panting, holding out a brown paper bag to them.

"I'm... sorry... this was... all that was left," the young man gasped between breaths.

Sebastian thanked him, slipped him a tip, and took the paper bag. The boy ran out of the gym, leaving Clay alone with Sebastian.

Sebastian plopped the bag onto the bench between them and opened it to peer inside. He sighed and rolled his eyes before Clay's curiosity got the better of him, yanking the costume out of the bag. A reindeer outfit dangled from a hanger, a bright red nose pinned to the unitard. He pulled out the antler headband with his opposite hand.

"Guess I'd better get changed," Clay said, resigned to his fate. He knew he'd be a laughingstock. Even the elf costume was better than *this*. But in the end, they were making kids happy. Sebastian abruptly stepped out of his Santa pants, handing them to Clay.

"Here," he said casually, standing in his boxer-briefs. He snatched the costume from Clay, shoved it into the paper bag and stalked off to the showers. Clay smirked and peeled the too-tight elf costume off, replacing it with the Santa costume. Once his suspenders were in place, Sebastian trudged out of the showers.

Clay immediately doubled over in laughter. Sebastian's obnoxiously thick muscles strained against the fabric. A small patch of beige fur was glued to his pecs and around his wrists. Sebastian glared at Clay and crossed his arms.

"Jesus Christ, we can swap. You look like Santa's hit man," Clay squeaked out between fits of laughter. Sebastian growled and stomped past him, aggressively donning his antlers. He turned to Clay as he fitted the red nose on.

"Let's just do this thing," he turned on his heel, striding out the door, his fluffy deer's tail bobbing after him. Clay broke down into hysterics once more before wiping the tears from his eyes, securing his beard and hat, then stepped out to greet the masses.

# Chapter 11

## Zamboni

There were too many humans.

Zamboni typically got nervous in this type of situation. Many humans meant many hands, all scrambling to touch him. He shrunk against Krystal's leg while she introduced him to the town council. They cooed over him and whispered baby talk. He sat his rump down and tilted his head, tongue lolling anxiously.

While the crowds were overwhelming, the air smelled delicious. Cinnamon, chocolate, peppermint, pine, and holly berries all mingled in the brisk evening air. Krystal guided him to another tent, chatting with another female. Zamboni's eye was captivated by a spinning wheel that made a loud clicking noise with each rotation. Still enthralled by the wheel, Zamboni hadn't noticed the giant deer-man beside him.

Zamboni's usual goofy grin disappeared, his tail drooping. He was unsure if this creature was a threat. It looked down at him dismissively and jumped into Krystal and the other female's conversation. Zamboni was still on the alert, but Krystal's relaxed posture lowered his hackles.

"Miss Simmons, so nice to meet in person." The deer-man offered his gloved hoof-hand and greeted Krystal with a hand belatedly.

"Mr. Rivera, is that you under that red nose?" Miss Simmons smiled prettily as the deer-man's heart quickened in nervousness. He yanked the ball from his nose. Zamboni's ears perked. Was he going to throw that?

"Ah, you got me! I apologize for interrupting your conversation, but I'm on a short break from our booth and don't have much time. Is it alright if we could discuss the possibility of working together on a long-term income booster for the casino? Extra tax dollars would surely help out the community, as I'm sure you're aware." Deer Man's antlers slid a bit forward on his head before he hastily readjusted them.

"Mr. Rivera, as I'm sure you're aware, I have been working closely with Mr. Emerson and his team to generate a larger income. I've been very pleased with their efforts, thus far." Miss Simmons' words had a bit more bite to them now. Deer Man's shoulders drooped, and he nodded, pulling out a card.

"I completely understand. However, if you change your mind, give me a call. The Rivera name has ties with many large corporations."

"Thank you, Mr. Rivera. I will take your offer under consideration." With a stern nod, Deer Man ambled off into the crowd.

"Oh, my god!" Krystal snorted and fell into hysterics. "That costume!"

Zamboni hopped up on his paws, tail wagging. He barked and put his paws on her belly. He loved it when Krystal laughed. It sounded like tinkling bells and hopefulness. Krystal bid the lady goodbye and circled them back around to yet another tent. To Zamboni's surprise, Deer Man was there, allowing children to see a fat man in a jacket.

Deer Man signaled to the line of people and mentioned a break. Several disappointed children whined. The bearded fat man stood and hopped over to Zamboni and Krystal.

"So, this is our new opponent, huh?" The man removed his face fur, which disturbed Zamboni immensely. He sat and plastered his ears to his skull. The man seemed kind enough, offering him a tiny piece of a granola hunk and let Zamboni scent him. "You're such a handsome fella." He asked Krystal if he could pet him. Why he couldn't ask *him* was beyond Zamboni's understanding.

When Krystal nodded, the man scratched the sensitive spot behind his ear. He smelled nice. Lemon and soap. Deer Man watched from behind, eyes studying the man curiously. Much as Zamboni wanted to be skeptical of the fat man, he had magical fingers. Zamboni wagged his tail, thumping it against the concrete.

When the man's hands pulled back, Zamboni immediately regretted ever suspecting the fat man. He and Deer Man took their leave, allowing Krystal and Zamboni to set up. His owner put a jangly collar on him along with a strange covering on his head. It was long and would occasionally bump into the side of his face. Soon, children were lining up to pat him for being a good boy. His tail thumped in overdrive.

At some point, Krystal lost the end of the leash during a paper shuffle. Zamboni's ears pointed, feeling the sudden slack. He stood to his paws, glanced over his shoulders at a wide-eyed Krystal, and bounded through the crowd. His heart pounded, the wind rushed through his fur. He rarely got the chance to run at full speed. He'd been feeling cooped up, but now all of his pent up energy had a release.

Shouts began behind him, the sound of pounding feet shortly joining them. He ran even faster, thrilled by the chase. Zamboni was circling the perimeter when suddenly Deer Man was before him, huffing. He was not wearing his deerskin now, which gave Zamboni pause.

"Easy boy." Deer Man slowly approached him, palms up. Zamboni turned on his back paws to escape, but a smaller man... the fat man, but not so fat now, was closing in on him. "Coming your way, Emerson," Deer Man shouted before lunging for Zamboni.

He missed by a hair and Zamboni intended to barrel into the approaching Non-Fat Man when the yank of the leash caused him to falter. Zamboni made one more mad dash and pulled Deer Man along after him. The sudden forward motion propelled Deer Man directly into Non-Fat Man. The two slammed together, promptly tangled in Zamboni's leash... which was still attached to his collar. He tumbled along with the men into a messy heap.

Non-Fat Man groaned. "Ow... why are you so damn heavy?"

"Sorry. I work out a lot. Muscle weighs more than fat and all that." Deer Man was able to prop an elbow into the grass to relieve pressure on Non-Fat Man.

"Christ, do you bench press Subarus and feast solely on protein?"

Deer Man snorted a laugh and shifted. He cursed and attempted to wiggle again.

"Bas, is that what I think it is?"

"I'm sorry... it's been a long time since I've... been intimate. I can't seem to get it *off* you. God, the world hates me."

"Popping a boner does *not* mean the world hates you. Gee, where are our rescuers? It's been a minute. Are we even that far out? Boy, Huskies run fast," Non-Fat Man rambled.

"Clay, why are you talking so much?"

"Because I am desperately trying not to pop a boner myself," Non-Fat Man said nervously. One of the men grunted and managed to unhook the leash from Zamboni's collar. Bystanders were enroute as he popped up from the pile. He sniffed Non-Fat Man's hair, which ended up costing him his freedom. The warm hands of Krystal looped around his neck and she pulled him from the fray. Several people rushed toward the tangled men to assist them.

"Good job, Zambo. There go our votes," Krystal sighed.

# CHAPTER 12

## Sebastian

"This is awkward," Sebastian muttered into Clay's ear as concerned townsfolk fled to their rescue. Clay giggled nervously and finally dislodged his perky ass from Sebastian's crotch. Well, that semi was firmly at full mast now. Clay offered Sebastian his hand, eyes urging him to hurry. The town's florist, Aster, was nearly at Clay's back. Sebastian took the offered hand and used Clay to block his majorly inconvenient erection.

"Wow, you guys sure took a tumble," Aster said, smirking at them.

"Yep," Clay chirped too loudly. Aster smiled fondly at Clay and patted him on the shoulder. "How've you been Clay? Mrs. Danvers always asks if I've seen you around."

Sebastian froze. Toby's mother. It was widely known she would leave sunflowers at Toby's grave every week. It made sense that Aster would often come into contact with her.

"Ah, yeah. I've been so busy with the race I haven't been able to make it to game night."

*Game night?* Sebastian looked Aster up and down. The guy was good looking and smiling way too fondly at Clay. Sebastian ground his molars.

"Well, let me know when your schedule frees up. We miss you."

"I will. Thanks for coming to our rescue," Clay purred. *Oh, hell no.* The erection was well and dead now. Sebastian stepped out from behind Clay, a furrow in his brow.

"Yeah, thanks man," Sebastian said gruffly. Did he just drop his voice an octave?

Aster's gaze fell on him, suddenly remembering his presence. He smiled nervously. "Any time!" Aster turned tail and made for his stall. Clay turned back to Sebastian, cheeks flushed.

"So, are you good now?" Clay's gaze flit down to his crotch and back up.

"Yeah. Thanks."

"Solidarity, brother."

Sebastian couldn't help but laugh. They waved off the onlookers and headed back down the hill toward the festival. "That was Aster, the florist, right? How did you two meet?"

"We met at a tree planting in town square not too long ago. I hadn't known him in school. He was a year behind us. Long story short, he invited me to his Dungeons and Dragons night. But it's been a while since I've been able to hang out."

"Yeah, I hear that. Kind of looking forward to all of this being behind me." Sebastian rubbed at the back of his neck, knowing there was tension there.

"You mean when I'm mayor and you're still Daddy's good little rich boy?" Clay batted his eyelashes innocently and Sebastian narrowed his eyes on him.

"We'll see about that."

Lately, Sebastian's evenings involved using his hand more than usual. He suspected it had something to do with the new redhead in his vicinity. Or maybe it was all the years of denying himself sexual gratification suddenly becoming too much to bear.

The air was getting quite brisk. Sebastian's breath puffed out in a warm cloud while he waited for his fake date outside the rink. He was scrolling through his social media, half a mind to look up said redhead, when a pair of furry boots stopped before him. He glanced up to find Clay, er... Ella. He was clad in a red wavy wig, an oversized tan cable-knit sweater, skinny jeans, and furry Chewbacca boots. He had a knit hat on with a huge furry pom-pom plopped on top. His makeup was done, and his cheeks were red.

"Well, don't you look cute."

"You should have seen my sister's face when I asked to borrow her clothes." Hearing him speak in his normal voice while dressed like a woman made Sebastian's mouth slope into a grin.

"Might want to mask your voice a little there, *Ella*."

"Right." He cleared his throat. "Bas! So nice to see you again. I absolutely adore hockey. How did you know?" Clay glommed onto Sebastian's arm, pressing the padded bra against him.

"Wait, why do you sound British?" Sebastian cocked an eyebrow at him.

"That's what happens when I try to alter my voice. I suppose it's nerves," he said with a flourish of his hand, accent in full effect.

"Well, at least you sound feminine. But before we go in… we should talk about…" Sebastian looked down pointedly at Clay's hands clinging to his arm. "PDA rules?"

"Hm, well…" Clay unlatched from his arm. "Are you comfortable with touching?"

"Yes. And I assume casual touching will be the linchpin in making this believable." Sebastian roped his arm around Clay's waist. "This okay?"

"Y-yes, that's okay… just no kissing." He looked down at his absurdly fluffy boots.

"Hate to break it to you, but we've kind of already done that."

"Yeah," he said, breaking character, "but now I know who you are." Sebastian's shoulders stiffened.

"Well, in any case, tonight will be simple. Get a few pictures snapped, stay until halftime at least, and then we can hammer out the details of your weird British background," he said gruffly. Clay agreed with a small nod. Sebastian's arm was still around his waist, so he tugged him forward into the ice rink.

They walked in from the cold to the much colder rink. The air inside was icicle sharp. Clay immediately hissed in surprise.

"I take it you've never been to a hockey game," Sebastian smirked, his fingers flexing involuntarily on Clay's waist.

"No, not quite." Clay started the accent up. "I'm afraid I may have dressed too lightly."

"Let's grab some popcorn and find our seats," Sebastian said, tugging Clay along to a fairly short popcorn line. Once Sebastian's buttery treat and Clay's hot roasted nuts—because of course—had been acquired, they made their way through the slew of fellow spectators. Some recognized him and called out his name. He'd wave in acknowledgement, but was sure not to leave Clay's side. After all, if this was a real date, he'd never abandon them to schmooze with voters.

They found a fairly empty space on the bleachers near the press. Sebastian was hoping they'd see him there without having to make a scene. Luckily for him, a scene was always sure to present itself.

"Sebby?" His mother's voice echoed off the ice even in the din of the fans.

"Oh, fuck." He looked down at Clay, who raised an eyebrow at him. "It's my parents... uh... okay I guess we're going to have to improv."

"Bas," Clay hissed, "just let me do the talking."

"Sebastian? Is that you, dear?" Essie Rivera's voice was undeniable. Several heads were turning in their direction already. Sebastian gritted his teeth and abruptly stood up.

"Mom. Not the best time." He hoped his voice wasn't as dismissive as he feared it may be. Essie scrunched her eyes at him, mouth pursed, until her eyes fell on the person beside him.

"Oh, I'm sorry sweetie, were you on a date?" Essie sized his date up while pretending to be bashful. To Sebastian's surprise, Clay stood and offered his hand.

"You must be Mrs. Rivera! Bas has told me so much about you," Clay said in his British lilt.

"I'm afraid I haven't a clue as to who you may be." Essie looked between Sebastian and Clay until recognition filled her eyes. *Shit shit shit shit.* "You must be the girl from the article in the paper!"

"That's me," Clay said, feigning sheepishness, "I'm Ella Chapman."

"Are you British?" Sebastian prayed for a stray puck to shatter his temple.

"I am. Lived near Castle Combe most of my life."

"Oh, how lovely! Such a beautiful town." Sebastian knew his mother was full of crap. She hadn't been outside the states since before moving to Wellsprings. But Essie was the slam dunk. What Sebastian was worried about was the imposing man who had finally reached his wife, holding two beers.

"Sebastian." Victor nodded to his son, handing Essie her beverage. "I see I missed the introductions."

"Dad, this is Ella Chapman. I believe I mentioned her." Clay stepped forward and offered his hand again.

"So nice to meet you, Mr. Rivera." Clay had a thousand-watt smile loaded, but Victor was as good as a dead fish when it came to small talk. He nodded to Clay, ignored the offered hand, and sat on the bleacher, nursing his overpriced beer. Essie followed suit, quietly sipping her beer and judging.

Sebastian pulled Clay onto the bench and stuffed popcorn in his mouth, hoping the saltiness would burn away the awkwardness. Clay must have sensed it was no-talking-time and focused on the roasted nuts and watched the ice resurfacer circle the rink. Mostly, Sebastian's parents left them alone, save for surreptitious glances. A few cameras were scanning the crowd now. This was Sebastian's chance.

"Brace yourself," he mumbled to Clay before roping his muscular arm around his shoulders. Clay jolted slightly when Sebastian leaned in and pressed his lips against Clay's cheek. Sebastian pulled back and grinned at his "date." Clay's furious blush gave him pause. Clay gently pushed him away, appearing coquettish.

"I said no kissing," he said in his breathy British voice. He was smiling, but his eyes were angry.

"Thought you meant on the lips. But I apologize. Won't happen again," Sebastian said through his grin. Clay coldly turned his attention back to the ice. Mercifully, the game chose that moment to start.

Sebastian hoped his face looked jovial because, on the inside, he was seething. *Jesus, does he really hate me that much?*

Twenty minutes in and two goals down, Wellsprings was in the lead against the neighboring town high school. Sebastian allowed himself to get lost in the quick pace of the players and ignore the man in drag beside him.

Finishing his popcorn, he stood to toss the bag into a nearby trash bin. He took Clay's empty nut pouch, *hah*, and noticed his hands were trembling. In fact, his entire body was shaking. Sebastian gritted his teeth, threw out the trash, and rushed back to plop on the bench. He opened his trench coat and hesitantly tucked Clay under his arm.

Clay was freezing. He let out a sigh of relief once the warmth from Sebastian's body wormed its way past Clay's sweater.

"Thank you," he whispered, nuzzling deeper into the coat. Sebastian smiled to himself and caught his dad staring at them... almost proudly. Sebastian frowned back at him, knowing full well what his dad's expression was saying, *"See? Look how straight you are. I knew you were punking me about the gay thing."*

Sebastian focused on the game for the rest of the time. When halftime rolled around, Clay said he wouldn't mind staying for the remainder of the game because he was actually enjoying it. No one was more surprised than Sebastian. If he recalled, Clay had referred to football as "sports ball."

"Oh? Big hockey nut?" Sebastian raised an eyebrow in defiance.

"I'm allowed to change opinions, you know," Clay said in his loud British voice. A few heads turned their way again. Sebastian could swear he saw a camera flash. *Good. The plan is working.*

He had to look charming, which was usually an arduous task for him if it wasn't a political function. He smiled saucily and snaked his arm around Clay's waist, pulling him tight to his side.

"Cameras are on us. Pretend you like me," he whispered dangerously close to Clay's ear. He could smell the *Irish Spring* soap clinging to his skin and the fresh smell of laundry. Underneath all that, Sebastian smelled a hint of tangy lemon. It would only take him moving an inch to lick his neck. Sebastian reared back abruptly, lest he do something he regretted.

Clay quickly put on his acting hat and leaned his head on Sebastian's shoulder. "Oh, I do love watching high schoolers brutalize each other on icy surfaces. What interesting things you like, Bas."

His own smile blindsided Sebastian, and he snorted a laugh. "Oh, Ella, whatever will I do with you?"

# Chapter 13

## Clay

He immediately peeled himself from Sebastian's side once the final buzzer erupted. Clay breathed deeply, hoping to calm his erratic pulse. There was no way touching Sebastian Rivera should feel that good. When he'd kissed his cheek, Clay had nearly gone into cardiac arrest. Just thinking about that night in the bar and how Sebastian's lips tasted was enough to ejaculate himself into the stratosphere.

*Get it together, Emerson. Sebastian Rivera is a bully... er, sort of. He's your political rival,* the logical part of his brain screamed.

*But he's also fucking hot and not quite as mean as you thought,* said his cock.

*FUCK ME!!!* That one was his butthole.

"Ready to go, Ella?" Sebastian was standing before him. Clay glanced around to see that a majority of the crowd had already exited the rink. Essie and Victor Rivera were suspiciously taking their time to gather themselves. *Shit.*

Clay stood and channeled all his inner *Bridgerton*. "Yes, let's." Clay braced himself before folding his arm around Sebastian's meaty forearm. All Clay could think about was taking his wig off. He was itchy as hell. He'd have to change and go straight to Cameron's to give her back the outfit.

The hunk of man he stood beside stilled when they stepped outside. Sebastian turned his head to glance over his shoulder and quickly ushered them into the closest store, which ended up being an ice cream parlor.

"Uh... want some ice cream?" Sebastian asked while glancing over his shoulder. His parents slowly passed by the windows, obviously watching. Clay took Sebastian's hand and led him over to check the display case.

"You know, after spending three hours at an ice rink, stopping for ice cream right after is not a typical choice." Clay smiled sweetly at him and relaxed his cheek muscles once the Riveras were gone.

"I know. I panicked," Sebastian said. The employee behind the counter was looking at him expectantly. "Uh, can I have a small potato chip?" Sebastian pulled out his wallet in a huff.

"Potato chip ice cream?" Clay was aghast.

"What? I like salty things."

"I bet you say that to all the boys," Clay whispered conspiratorially, dropping his voice and wiggling his eyebrows. Sebastian theatrically rolled his eyes.

"Whatever. Do you want something?"

"Nah, all froze up, thanks." Clay was getting tired of masking his voice. He'd have to break character soon. Sebastian nodded and asked the cashier for it to go instead. He paid, slipped a five in the tip jar, and ushered Clay outside.

"Did you walk here?"

"Yes... are you offering to drive me home?" Clay batted his fake eyelashes. He most certainly did *not* want to walk in the cold after being cold for several hours.

"Maybe. I parked around the back of the rink, just in case you needed a break."

Clay looked around them, thankful to see the street abandoned. "Thank god... I wasn't sure how much longer I could keep talking like that," he said, reverting to his natural voice. Sebastian's car came into view as they rounded the arena - a silver Lexus, of course. The two hopped in and Sebastian blasted the heat. Clay sighed and sunk into the plush—heated—leather seats.

Clay rattled off his address and Sebastian swiftly slipped on to the road. *Damn, this thing rides nice.* Clay closed his eyes to avoid having to speak with him.

"Thank you again for doing this, Clay."

"Thank you for funding my program, Bas." Clay cracked a lid and saw Sebastian's face shift from neutral to grump. After ten minutes of driving in silence, Sebastian pulled up to Clay's apartment building.

"Huh," Sebastian said with surprise.

"What?" Clay was quickly unbuckling his seat belt.

"I live in the apartment building behind yours."

"Of course you do. Fucking small town. Well, thanks for the ride," Clay was rolling out of the car when Sebastian called out "I'll text you!" through the closed door. Clay rolled his eyes, walking up the walkway. His eyes focused on the kid sitting beside the call buttons. The lanky purple hair stopped Clay in his furry-booted tracks. Charlie's eyes were wide, mouth hanging open.

"Uncle Clay?"

"Charlie, let's go inside."

Clay calmly unlocked the door to the building and took his nephew's hand to guide him to his apartment. Once the apartment door had locked behind them, Clay pulled off his wig and faced his nephew.

"Charlie, what are you doing here? Does your mom know you're here?"

"What?! Wait, what the hell are you wearing? Are those Mom's boots?!"

Clay sighed and relayed the story while he stripped out of the clothes.

"Isn't Sebastian Rivera your rival?"

"Yes. But he's agreed to help fund a project for me." He was in his boxers, folding his arms across his chest. "Okay, so now you know my deal. Why are you on my doorstep?"

"I have so many more questions... but I wanted to talk to you."

"Sure, Char. Make yourself comfortable while I get dressed. And text your mom before she calls the police."

While Clay was throwing on sweats and a long sleeve shirt, his phone dinged. Charlie must have texted Cameron.

Cameron

Is he ok? Y is he there???

I'll find out and let you know.

R u bringing my boots back???

I assumed the return of your son was more important than your yeti boots, but I will return both later.

She responded with two thumbs up emojis. Clay was about to shove the phone into his pocket, but he noticed there was an unread message from Sebastian. He clicked it open far too quickly. He blushed in the empty room over his eagerness.

Sebastian

> Hey. I was thinking we could do dinner and a movie on Thursday.

> That way, you don't have to talk in that terrible English accent the whole time.

> You're just in awe of my raw, indisputable talents.

> I'm not sure that's it… so is that a yes for Thurs?

> Yeah.

Clay chucked his phone onto the duvet and went to speak with his nephew. Charlie was in his kitchen, elbow deep in a Cheez-It box. Clay laughed and moved to the fridge to pull out two cans of soda.

"Alright, Char. Tell me what's going on." The two were sitting on Clay's couch, colas in hand.

"Well… I think I like someone."

"What's their name?"

"His name is Brennan," Charlie said, nervously turning his soda in his palms.

"So, you came all this way just to dish on hot boys?"

"No, not exactly. He's sort of… my bully."

"What?!" Unbidden images of Clay's own high school torment flashed behind his eyes. He absently rubbed at his forearms.

"I know. I know. But he's such a tsundere. He's been nice to me in between the bullying. We watched *Jujutsu Kaisen* together."

"Charlie. Just because someone watches anime with you does not mean that behavior is healthy. It's toxic. We've spoken about you reading these bully romances... if Brennan is bullying you, report it."

Charlie scrunched up on the couch, leveling a cold stare at his uncle. *Uh oh, he's about to shut down.* Clay sighed and patted Charlie's foot.

"Okay, I get it. I'll back off. You know I'm only trying to protect you."

"I know, Uncle Clay."

"Just promise me, if things get out of hand, you'll do the right thing. High school can be hell for queer kids." Clay looked away from his nephew. Unwanted memories flooded his mind.

"So, it's true?" Charlie's voice was small, but it snapped Clay to attention.

"What's true?"

"The rumors. They say a gay kid killed himself in the auditorium because he was bullied so badly."

"Char—"

"His boyfriend found him, and he was so upset that he slit his wrists, but he did it wrong..." Charlie's eyes drifted to his uncle's wrists and Clay quickly folded his arms against his chest. "Uncle Clay—"

"Let's get you home, kiddo." Clay pulled himself off the couch to yank on sneakers. He busied himself looking for a bag to carry his sister's clothes in to avoid thinking about his greatest shame. He could feel Charlie's eyes on him as he flitted around the room. His nephew begrudgingly readied himself to make the trek home.

They left for the twenty-minute walk to Cameron's. The chilly air embraced their exposed flesh, causing the pair to focus on rushing to warmth. It left little room for speaking. Charlie kept his eyes on the ground for a good portion of their walk. When they were about two-thirds of the way there, Charlie grabbed his uncle's icy hand.

"I'm sorry, Uncle Clay. I understand why you're so against bullying. I promise you I won't put myself in danger."

Clay sighed and pulled his nephew against his side, ruffling his lanky purple hair. "That's all I ask, Char. I love you."

"I love you too, Uncle Clay."

# CHAPTER 14

## Sebastian

He'd been waiting for thirty minutes. The waiter graciously gave him an extra basket of breadsticks after he'd eaten the entire first. He checked his phone again, hesitating over the keyboard. He chickened out and flipped it on its face on the table.

Sebastian knew he'd sent the correct details... he'd already checked ten times. A seething cloud of anger coiled around him. He cursed, standing from the table to flag down the waiter for the check, when Clay burst through the doors. His wig was disheveled, and he appeared more than rushed.

"You're late," Sebastian growled as Clay collapsed into his chair.

"I know. Bit of a wardrobe malfunction. My sister wasn't exactly keen on giving me more clothes, so I had to pick the most androgynous things I owned," he said in a hushed English voice. Clay wore skinny jeans, a pair of scuffed Chuck Taylors, and a flouncy white shirt with lantern sleeves. He pointed to his shirt. "This is a pirate shirt from four Halloweens ago."

"You *do* know how to text people, right?" Sebastian was still grumpy about his tardiness. Clay's eyes narrowed at Sebastian's domineering tone.

"I knew I should've just canceled." Clay stood, the chair scraping loudly against the tile. Several diners glanced their way. Sebastian caught Clay's hand in a panic.

"I'm sorry. Please stay." Clay leveled a devastating glare at him but slowly sunk down into the chair.

"You're lucky I'm hungry." Clay helped himself to the breadsticks while the waiter appeared to take their orders. They quickly ordered, each barely glancing at the menu. When the waiter flitted away, Sebastian warily watched as Clay aggressively bit into another breadstick.

"So... shall we talk logistic–"

"My nephew knows."

"Oh... well, he's what? Fifteen? I'm not really worried about rumors from kids." Sebastian shrugged and picked up another breadstick. Clay blinked a moment and put his bread down, accent gone.

"No, not about the agreement... well, he does, but that's not what I'm talking about." Clay pulled his pirate sleeves up to reveal his scars. "He knows. About my past. About what happened to Tobias... all of it." He shoved his sleeves back down. "The stupid kids talk about it like it was a goddamn urban legend." Clay put his head in his hands. "My nephew is bisexual, and he's already been getting bullied... now he knows just how cruel they can be. I'm so scared for him." Clay's voice cracked. Sebastian reached a hand out to comfort him, but he hesitated, knowing Clay wouldn't want his comfort. He dropped his hand and hung his head.

"I'm sorry. That must be difficult." Sebastian cringed at his own words. *You fucking shit.*

"Difficult. Hah! You really are a poet, Bas." Clay unclasped his head and raked his fingers through the wig. Their food came and saved Sebastian from wrecking the evening further. They barely spoke during dinner. Clay was lost in his thoughts and Sebastian was actively trying *not* to think about things. Reminiscing typically led him to spiraling emotions.

"Hey, what do you say we skip the movie and go shopping for some outfits for you? My treat. You can even get, what did you say... androgynous styles so you can wear them whenever."

Clay glanced up, the ghost of a smile playing on his lips. "Okay. That sounds nice. But I'll need some footwear, too."

"Of course." Sebastian smirked and cut into his steak.

"Okay, this is a little bit insane. I don't need fifty outfits, Bas," Clay whispered as Sebastian handed his credit card to the cashier.

"Think of it as payment for your time. It really is not a problem." Sebastian signed the receipt and looped the shopping bags on his arms. Clay rolled his eyes.

"Yeah, keep rubbing it in, Rich Boy."

"Oh... well if you feel that way, I'll cancel the limo."

"Limo?" Clay batted his fake lashes. Sebastian laughed and pointed at the waiting limousine across the street.

"I figured we could just ride around and have some drinks. You can let your hair down. Have a little ice breaker."

Clay regarded him with sparkling green eyes. Sebastian could see gratitude there. The driver, who happened to be Marc, opened the back door for them. Marc helped Sebastian with the bags as Clay climbed in.

"She's cute, Bas," Marc said under his breath. Sebastian rolled his eyes at his friend and climbed in to join Clay. He waited for Marc to return to the driver's seat before taking the seat beside the partition window.

"Around the town, please, Jeeves. I'll let you know when to stop."

"Fuck you, Bas—" Sebastian closed the partition, cutting off Marc's sentence. Sebastian sighed loudly and settled beside the bar, pulling the chilled champagne from the ice bucket. He popped the cork and poured two glasses. Reaching across, he handed one to Clay.

Clay smiled and pulled the wig off, running fingers through his helmeted hair, causing it to stick up at odd angles. Sebastian tried to focus on his champagne and not on how cute his political rival looked. Clay took a sip from his glass before using a napkin to wipe the makeup from his face. He unclasped the padded bra and yanked it out from under his shirt, sighing in relief.

"I do not envy women," he said as he pitched the bra into one of the bags. Clay unbuttoned a couple of the top buttons of the pirate shirt, allowing a few auburn chest hairs to poke out. Sebastian bit the inside of his lip, hoping to not lose control. He grunted in response, finished his champagne, and poured another glass.

Clay drained his glass and held the flute out for a refill. "So, ice breakers, right? What's your favorite color?"

"Yes, Clay. Because knowing my favorite color is the most important information about me."

"You joke, but colors are very important in judging compatibility."

"Yeah, sure they are. What's yours then?"

"Green. So? I showed you mine."

"People always tease me about it." Clay stared at him expectantly, glass clasped in both hands. He sighed. "It's brown. More specifically, terracotta." Clay nearly did a spit-take.

"Brown? Interesting." He looked away, eyes shifty. "Green and brown are complimentary."

"And what exactly does that mean?" Sebastian poured another glass for himself. The champagne was warming his skin. Clay finished his and handed his glass to Sebastian for another refill. Clay's cheeks were tinted pink, his freckles dotting the flush.

"It means," he said, fidgeting with his hands, "it means we're soul-mates."

Sebastian choked on his drink. He coughed, sticking the bottle back in the ice. Once he caught his breath, he leveled a shaky gaze on Clay.

"Is that so?"

Clay chewed on his lip, and sighed. When he met Sebastian's eyes again, a twitch of his mouth broke into a full out grin.

"Nah, I'm full of shit." Clay laughed while Sebastian grimaced at him. "Whew, I think I may be getting drunk." Clay giggled to himself. Sebastian couldn't help but smirk, that is until his father called. He apologized to Clay and took the call.

"Hi, Dad."

"Son!" The background noise was deafening, and his father sounded about four Old Fashions in. "I was thinking. Does Ella want to come to Thanksgiving? She's from Britain, right? Surely, she doesn't have plans to celebrate."

"Thanksgiving?" Sebastian's voice rose an octave, rewarded by a curious glance from Clay. He stood and moved beside Sebastian, trying to listen in. "We agreed on Sunday dinner at the end of the month. That's even less time."

"Ah, well, you two seemed to be hitting it off. Bring her."

"I'll see if she's available—" Sebastian said before Victor hung up. Sebastian seethed a moment before turning to Clay. "So..."

"I'll let Cameron know to save me a plate." Sebastian's shoulders slumped in relief. "On one condition." The tension was back in his shoulders.

"Shoot."

"Give me the rest of that bottle," Clay stage whispered and pointed to the champagne. Sebastian snorted and handed it to him. Clay enthusiastically abandoned all appearances of decorum and drank straight from the bottle. Sebastian found some cold beers in the mini fridge and made quick work of those. He was certainly feeling woozy when Clay suggested twenty-one questions.

"Okay, I'll go first. Why did you enter the mayoral race?" Clay batted his eyes and upended the bottle. It had been empty for five minutes, but he seemed determined not to waste a single drop.

"Parents made me. My turn. Why don't you see your parents for Thanksgiving? Don't they live a couple towns over?" To Clay's delight, Sebastian pulled the spare champagne from the mini fridge.

"Wow. Starting off strong. Okay, well, they were very *opinionated* regarding my sexuality. It was toxic, and I cut them out of my life. Cameron always stood by my side. She was disgusted by them, and now we are each other's only family.

"I'm sorry you had to go through that."

"No worries, it's in the past. I'm better off." Clay waved off the idea. "Okay, so it's my turn. What was your dream job before politics?"

"Hm... I suppose a chef. I was interested in learning how to make Puerto Rican dishes." Sebastian had always wanted to travel the world and taste all the different manners of cuisine. But most importantly, he wanted to visit his home country.

"Don't you like… eat them all the time, though? I assume you have a general idea."

"No… anyway, it's my turn. You're breaking your own rules." Clay raised his arms in surrender. "Okay… at the ice rink. You said no kissing. Why?"

"Um. Sexual harassment much? Jeez." Clay rolled his eyes and crossed his leg over his knee.

"This game was your idea," Sebastian said gruffly.

"Fine." Clay sighed loudly. "I rarely kiss guys. It's a little too intimate for me. I like to keep them at a safe distance." He glanced at him sidelong. "The kiss at the bar was a fluke… an earth shattering fluke."

"My god, am I that terrible a kisser?" Sebastian wilted slightly. Clay looked at him, aghast. He got in Sebastian's face, clearly fueled by the liquor.

"Are you stupid? That was the most amazing kiss of my fucking life, Bas. Like you should do a TED talk on kissing. It was that good." Clay's face was close. Sebastian could taste the champagne on his breath. His heart pounded in his ears. Before he could stop himself, most likely, alcohol fueled, his hand slid up the back of Clay's neck.

"Then how about one more fluke?" Sebastian's free hand cupped Clay's cheek while his thumb traced his bottom lip. Clay shuddered and drowned Sebastian with his emerald eyes.

"God, you're so corny." Clay closed the short distance and planted his lips on Sebastian's.

Sebastian groaned in approval and swiftly met Clay's tongue with his own. Fire licked between them, the joining of their mouths not enough. They ground against each other, begrudgingly leaving clothes in their way. Clay made happy muffled sounds as Sebastian's tongue plundered his mouth. He tried to suppress his need to touch him further, but he was merely a man, and was soon gripping Clay's perky ass through his skinny jeans.

Clay gasped and broke the kiss, pressing into Sebastian's greedy hands. Clay threw his head back and rubbed his obvious erection against Sebastian's leg, moaning enticingly. Through the sheer cotton pirate shirt, Clay's stiff pink nipples poked out. Sebastian licked his lips and descended upon them, sucking and biting through the shirt. Clay slid his fingers through Sebastian's thick hair and fisted, holding him there.

"Hey Bas, I got a call from your old man to pick him up from some party, ah, oh whoops! Sorry, my bad," Marc called through the partition as he swiftly closed it. Sebastian and Clay stared at each other, each trying to get their breathing under control. Clay cleared his throat and removed himself from Sebastian's lap. He rearranged the bulge in his skinny jeans and threw his wig back on.

"How much do you think he saw?" Clay asked calmly as he gathered the bags from their shopping spree.

"P...probably not much," he stammered out, trying to ignore his own arousal. Sebastian knocked on the partition and told Marc to pull down the next block. They were miraculously close to their apartments.

When the limo came to a stop, Clay burst through the door, several bags in tow. He popped his head back inside. "Thanks for tonight, Bas. Text you later." He was cold and emotionless as he shut the door behind him. Sebastian watched him scurry into the building like his ass was on fire. Still breathless, Sebastian dropped his head into his hands.

"Fuck," he whispered to the empty limousine.

# Chapter 15

## Clay

"Wait, *that's* why you borrowed my clothes last week?" Cameron asked, appalled, as she reached past a dawdling customer to grab a Pumpkin Pecan Waffle candle. She tossed it into Clay's basket while he smelled the seasonal body wash scent.

"I knew you wouldn't believe me. How could you?" Clay flagged down an employee to ask if they had a box set for the scent he was holding. The frazzled teen excused herself to the back room in a flurry of blue gingham. The holiday shopping season was in full swing in Wellsprings—very on brand.

Retail employees were ragged and quitting at the drop of a hat, only to get the same position at a neighboring store a week later. Stores boasted Pre-Pre-Black Friday Sales. People were cranky, towing equally cranky children behind them. The perfect backdrop to drop the atom bomb he'd been keeping in his back pocket on his sister.

"I mean... my gaydar is pretty good. Rivera never even registered a blip." Cameron propped a hand on her hip, pouting full force. Clay mentally rolled his eyes. *Cameron and her gaydar.*

"He was pretty deep in the closet. He claims he isn't now, but I don't think he even realizes how hard he tries to present as straight. His parents messed him up." The employee finally returned with a boxed set, dodging between the crowded aisles. Clay thanked her and slipped a ten-dollar bill into her hand. She paused and smiled genuinely at him before being pulled away by an impatient mother of two screaming toddlers.

The siblings made their way to the new cologne display, obnoxiously spraying the sample bottles on each other's arms and inhaling. One scent had the hair on the back of his neck standing on end. It sent shivers up his spine as it brought a certain burly man to mind. Clay responded by simply placing it in his basket. Maybe he would spray it on his pillows.

"I still don't understand why you agreed to go to Thanksgiving. That's a lot of pressure." Cameron ushered a slew of hand sanitizers into her perilously full basket as they headed for the registers.

"I know. It was a part of the agreement... and I'm not backing out if I can get this program off the ground." The two parted, going to their respective cashiers, paid, and rejoined at the store's entrance. Clay took Cameron's bags from her and motioned to the cafe kiosk nearby. Cameron sunk into a chair, cradling her swollen belly as she did. Clay grabbed their two drinks and settled among their myriad of bags. Picking up where they left off, Cameron settled a stern gaze on him.

"I know how passionate you are about the bully program, but is it worth the cost of your soul?"

Clay blanched. "What do you mean?"

"I mean, he's asking you to dress in drag in front of his family. That's fucked up, Clay."

"We're just faking. It's not like I don't have fun doing drag from time to time. I'm just going to treat this as a foray into acting." He flourished his hand about, trying desperately not to let her words sting. To avert attention from him, he asked, "How has Charlie been doing?"

His sister raised a single eyebrow, clearly noting the subject change. "Oh, more of the same. He's thinking about changing his hair color to pink now. I don't understand why he feels the need to cover up his beautiful red hair." Apart from Colby, everyone in the Emerson bloodline had natural red hair. "Soooo, when's your next date? Sorry... I mean acting practice."

"Tomorrow. We're trying to lay some groundwork on a background story. Not. A. Date."

"Oh, shut up with your non-committal bullshit. It *so* is. Are you going to jump him again?" Cameron smiled slyly at him. He fixed a glare on his sister. Why had he even told her about the limo?

"Absolutely not." Clay could still taste Sebastian's tongue. "Alcohol certainly isn't doing us any favors, so we're going to a casual coffee meeting to study." He and Sebastian had ignored each other for the week, skipping their last appointment. Neither had the courage to meet face to face after that night. When Bas finally texted him to meet up for coffee, Clay was relieved he didn't have to be the one to reach out.

"Study? Like getting to know each other?" Cameron hedged.

"Yeah. Exactly."

"So, a date."

"Oh, my god." Clay sighed and put his head in his hands. Cameron laughed and emphatically clapped her hands.

"This. Is. Rom. Com. Shit." She punctuated each word with a clap.

"You're the absolute worst."

"Maybe, but you love me." Cameron gave him a knowing smile before taking a sip of her decaf latte.

Sebastian was late.

An hour and thirteen minutes late, to be exact. Clay frowned at his phone screen, waiting for some kind of message to pop up. Nothing. Was this revenge for being late the first time? No. Not straight-laced Sebastian. He'd been stood up. Clay cursed and shoved his phone into his hoodie pocket. He quickly finished his latte and tossed the cup into the trash on his way out the door.

Clay was fuming. After they'd gone out of their way to make plans at a cafe outside of town, so Clay didn't have to be in disguise, the prick stood him up. The ever punctual, always practical, Sebastian Rivera hadn't so much as texted him to cancel. And after Sebastian reprimanded *him* for being late! The audacity. Clay was angry, baffled, and a little bit hurt... but mostly angry.

It wasn't until he was home in old Christmas pajama pants watching a Hallmark Christmas movie that his phone rang. Clay looked at it repulsively when Sebastian's name popped onto the screen. He answered with a, "Yeah?"

"I'm so sorry. Where are you right now?"

"Back at my apartment, because, you know, you never showed up."

"I'll explain when I get there."

"Get here?" Clay's voice came out as a squeak as he looked around the living room. A bare pre-lit Christmas tree sat in the corner, un-opened totes of ornaments and decorations sat piled in front of it.

There were more than a few empty wine bottles and the like strewn about the kitchen island. "Um..."

"I'm at the entrance. Buzz me in. Please hurry. I don't need people to see me."

*Shit! Why did he have to live so close?*

"Okay, okay." Clay leapt up from the couch and danced over to the buzzer while plucking trash from the kitchen island. He buzzed Bas in and hung up, rushing around the apartment to stow things away that he didn't need Sebastian Rivera seeing. Like his sad Christmas pants with dancing Santas on them. *Fuck!*

A soft knock signaled his arrival and Clay jumped over the couch, clicking Hallmark off and pulling on a hoodie before opening the door. He attempted to look put out and ushered Sebastian in. The man smelled wildly enticing as he whisked by. He wore a sweater and jeans, a scarf loosely looped around his neck, peacoat unbuttoned. Clay pointed at the coat rack tucked in the corner and flounced over to the totes of decorations, making a show of plugging in the tree and opening the top tote, as if he was doing this all along and not moping on the couch watching garbage holiday television in November.

Sebastian hovered on the outskirts of the tote barricade between him and Clay. He frowned and shuffled his feet, nervously glancing around Clay's apartment.

"Ah, so... about the cafe," Bas started, rubbing the back of his neck.

"I'm listening," Clay said as he unspooled gold garland from a box. He was tucking the garland into the branches when Sebastian cleared his throat.

"Clay," Bas said his name in a commanding voice. It sent shivers up Clay's spine. He struggled to keep the thought of Sebastian's mouth on his locked away. He begrudgingly looked over his shoulder to see

Sebastian standing on the opposite side of Clay's tote, arms folded. "I'd like your attention, please."

*Oh, Daddy. All you have is my attention.* Clay coughed, bidding his inner ho away. "You have my attention."

"Thank you. I couldn't make it because I was in a meeting. It ran much longer than anticipated."

"Okay... but there was no reason you couldn't shoot me a text to cancel."

"You're right. I should have communicated with you. But I was hoping to meet you with good news."

Clay sighed and handed Bas an ornament to hang while he finished stuffing the garland in. "I was meeting with the bank to see if I could access my trust fund. I wanted to start the process for your program. It can take a while to approve because my dad is still in charge of the account... even though I'm a grown ass adult." He said the last part through his teeth. "I had to call my attorney to check the legality. Unfortunately, it's perfectly legal for him to have control over a thirty-year-old's money. But Dad said he'd approve the withdrawal... if I make good on our deal to go to Thanksgiving."

"So, we really gotta sell this, huh?"

"Yes... and I wanted to discuss this with you. It may require... kissing. Or I should say, public kissing."

"Jesus," Clay whispered under his breath. "I understand where you're coming from... if it's for the good of the program, it's fine with me." Sebastian stoically nodded and plucked more ornaments from the box. Clay smiled tensely and put on some Christmas music while they decorated. When they were ready to add the star, Clay handed it to Sebastian.

"Clearly, I'm too short." Clay pouted up at him and Sebastian threw him a heart-stopping, lopsided smile. Clay's heart thundered, and he put distance between them again, busying himself with decorating the rest of the apartment. After securing the star, Sebastian trailed after him, taking Clay's orders dutifully.

Two hours passed and Clay offered to order them pizza. Sebastian cracked the beer Clay tossed him and took a long swallow. Clay certainly wasn't watching the way Bas's Adam's apple bobbed. Nope. He wasn't.

The pizza arrived just as they finished laying the last of the decor out. Clay quickly stowed the empty tote bins in his hall closet and padded to the kitchen to dish out their food.

Pizza and beers in hand, the two awkwardly sat around Clay's kitchen island. Surprisingly, it was Sebastian who spoke first.

"So your sister, Cameron, knows about our arrangement?"

"Yeah, but don't worry, she's a vault. Besides, she's too busy being obnoxiously pregnant."

"That's right, and you mentioned you had a nephew?" Something softened in Bas's honey eyes upon mentioning the kids. It was a look that reflected his own, Clay realized.

Clay pulled out his phone to show Sebastian a picture of his niece and nephew. "Yeah! That's Charlie and Clarissa. Cameron, who you know, and her husband, Colby."

"I might come across stupid, but I take it names starting with a 'C' is by design?"

"Yeah, old family tradition. Colby was a bonus, though. Cameron swears up and down that his name had nothing to do with falling in love with him. I call bullshit."

"Do you know the baby's name yet?"

"No. Cameron is being insufferable. She isn't finding out the baby's sex and withholding all name ideas. Never did that with the other two." Clay took another slice and handed one to Sebastian. "So, let's get down to business. A Rivera Thanksgiving. What am I walking into?"

Sebastian's shoulders tightened, and he put down his pizza. He quickly plucked another can of beer from the six-pack and drained half before speaking.

"Well, my Puerto Rican family is not in the states. So, it's mostly my parents' friends and co-workers. Basically, a bunch of rich old white people... no offense."

"None taken. How much affection are you expecting us to publicize?" Sebastian seemed surprised by the question. He rubbed the back of his neck, and a light flush tickled his cheeks.

"Depending on alcohol levels—both my father's and my own—it could be a few pecks."

"Your own, huh?"

"I can't usually handle family functions without the assistance of vodka." He hid his face behind his beer for a moment before continuing, "And I can be... affectionate when drunk. Especially if there's a cute boy nearby."

*Cute boy?! Be cool, Clay. Be coooool.*

"Hah! Same." *Oh, my god.*

Sebastian dragged his eyes to Clay's. He blinked a moment in what Clay assumed was confusion before picking up his paper plate and disposing of it in the trash bin.

"Well, I should be going. It's getting late and I have a rally tomorrow."

"Oh, yeah, I had one today, actually."

"How did it go?" Sebastian shrugged his peacoat on and lingered by the door. He pulled a decoration from the last pile and stretched up to poke it into the door frame with a thumbtack.

"We aren't supposed to talk about the race... but it went well. We did some Christmas caroling at the end. They ate it up."

"Good. I don't like an easy win." Sebastian smiled devilishly at him and unbolted the door. Clay scoffed and glanced above Bas's head. The decoration he'd put up was the mistletoe. When Sebastian realized what Clay was looking at, he went still. The two were unconsciously standing close, trading the same breath back and forth. Clay met Sebastian's eyes and could see the hesitation. The air sizzled between them and Clay had to bite the inside of his cheek to keep from closing the gap.

Bas sighed wistfully and cupped Clay's face in his large hand. Clay inhaled sharply, his nose flooding with Sebastian's sweet and musky cologne. Bas traced Clay's lower lip with his thumb while biting his own. Clay's fingertips grazed Bas's arm, a quiet invitation to continue. His skin was hot, his body quivering from the need to kiss the man in front of him. Clay leaned forward and was abruptly met with cold, empty air.

Sebastian had taken a huge step backward into the hallway. Clay blinked before straightening his spine. *Um, what the hell?*

"Sorry. I'll, er, see you," Sebastian said in a hurried grumble and rushed out of Clay's building. Clay stared after him, mouth slightly agape. He quietly shut the door and glanced at the wooden box, watching him from the nearby shelf. A heaviness settled between his shoulders as he found himself in front of it.

Clay slipped off the top and the gray eyes of Tobias stared into his own. Forever frozen in time at seventeen. A familiar lump lodged in Clay's throat. He picked up the picture. Toby smiled at him in the button down his mom had made him wear for picture day..

"I'm sorry, Toby. Will you forgive me if I let myself like him... just a little bit?" Tobias's unchanging face stared back, and Clay sighed deeply. He glanced down at the box and saw the hospital band. Old letters. Sketches. And nestled in the box's corner, the business card from the therapist Clay had seen afterward. He picked it up gingerly between his fingertips.

Maybe it was time to schedule his long overdue follow-up.

# Chapter 16

## Zamboni

He was nearing the den. A few more minutes of digging and he would be upon the sleeping chipmunks. This was it. He'd finally be able to protect his owner and the town from the tiny striped devils. Zamboni was sure he'd get a cookie for his trouble.

He could smell them before he broke through their dirt ceiling. The pungent rodents were all curled around each other, jerking awake from the sudden rush of brisk air. The chipmunks groggily ambled around, but once Zamboni let out a victory howl, they fully woke and scattered. He lunged at their speedy bodies but failed to catch a single one. The rodents streamed out from under his paws, using the pit he dug to escape. He backed out of the tunnel and took off in pursuit. The town square gardens were being overrun by a sea of chittering fuzz balls.

"Zambo," Krystal called as he whizzed by her, hot on a 'munk's tail. He snagged the little creature in his jaws, eliciting raucous squeals from the thing. It squirmed and bit at Zamboni's lips, but he wasn't about to relinquish his long-awaited prize.

"Zamboni!"

He turned at Krystal's harsh tone, ears pulled back. She looked furious with him.

"Drop it," she said in a commanding voice. Zambo whined, not wanting to let the offender go. "Drop. It." Zamboni huffed and lowered his muzzle to the grass, releasing the fighting critter. It skittered off, joining its brethren. "Good boy."

He tentatively wagged his tail. Krystal sighed and patted his head before clipping his leash on and leading him to the front of the gardens. The chipmunks were zipping in and out of bushes, still in a panic. A few humans were standing by, pointing their glass rectangles in the chipmunks' direction.

"Hey! It's mayoral candidate Zamboni! You found the chipmunks?" One of the humans approached. He smelled familiar and Zamboni realized it was the fence human. He wagged his tail and crouched in a play pose. The fence human pulled a cookie from his bag and tossed it to Zambo. He jumped and snatched it out of the air.

At least he'd gotten his cookie.

# Chapter 17

## Sebastian

He'd baked two sweet potato pies, three loaves of herby sour-dough, and several trays of cookies since leaving Clay's the day before. To say he was stressed was an understatement. A knock sounded at his door just as he finished moving his most recent batch of cookies to the cooling sheet.

He hollered for them to come in, only to come face to face with Marc. Sebastian jumped backward, brandishing his jumbo cookie spatula in defense.

"I can't believe you leave your door unlocked. Are you trying to get me fired?"

"I unlocked it ten minutes ago because I was expecting *you*. Besides, I don't need a bodyguard." Marc rolled his eyes at him and took a seat at the kitchen table. Sebastian had invited him over for lunch before the rally that evening. He needed to use up some of his baked goodies. The sweet potato pies he could freeze and bring to Thanksgiving. But the bread and cookies had to go.

He planned to make sandwiches with the bread and the cookies he supposed he could hand out to his campaign team. He started cutting into a loaf when Marc sighed.

"You're baking. Is something wrong?"

Sebastian glanced at his friend and wordlessly continued slicing the bread. He quickly assembled sandwiches for the two of them before joining him at the table. Marc quietly sipped the beer he'd been handed while continuing to watch him.

"Fine. Yes, something is bothering me." Sebastian bit into his sandwich, hoping that was the end of the conversation.

"It's about that redhead, isn't it?" Marc finally bit into his food while Sebastian choked on his. "I'm not stupid, Bas. You're into him."

"Him? Don't you mean her?" Sebastian could feel his body tighten in response.

"No," Marc simply said as he polished off his first half and regarded his friend somberly. "I know you're gay. I just don't know why you never told me." How could Marc know? He'd been careful for so long. "You've liked Clay Emerson since high school. It's not really a shock. And before you say anything, his drag's not *that* good."

Sebastian sputtered and took a moment to organize his thoughts. "I keep saying that I never tried to hide it… but that's a lie. You know how my parents are. You know what happened to Tobias. I was scared… and that fear never left me." Marc smiled gently and put his mammoth hand on Sebastian's shoulder.

"I understand. But this is a safe space. I love you and you can trust me."

Sebastian folded in on himself, a sob wrenching free from the prison where he'd kept all his big feelings. That control finally slipped, and the tears flowed freely. Marc pulled him into a hug and let Sebastian snot up his shirt. Once his tears were spent, Sebastian told him everything.

It left him weightless. Happy even, to have that off his chest to at least one person.

"Did you know I reported him? Jesse. I told the guidance counselor about the bullying twice. Before Tobias... well, they never took it seriously." Sebastian swiped aggressively at the tear tracks that had long since dried.

"Bas, you can't blame yourself for that. It's the school's fault for being negligent. At least they sent Jesse to prison. Hopefully, someone made him their bitch."

Sebastian grumbled and pinched the bridge of his nose. Talking about the past brought unwanted memories to the forefront of his mind. He let out a shaky sigh and let his newfound truth faucet run.

"I was the one who found Clay... and Tobias. I knew Clay was in the drama club and usually stopped by the theater on his breaks. I snuck in through the outside entrance to take a peek at him practicing. Then I saw the blood... then the swinging."

"Holy shit, Bas. I had no idea."

"It's still a blur. I remember running to Clay and ripping off pieces of my shirt to tie on his wrists. I know I carried him to the nurse's office. But I don't remember much else. The paramedics said if I hadn't tied those binds as tightly as I had... he might have died."

"Whoa... you saved his life. My god you're a hero, man!"

"Please don't say that."

"Does he know?"

Sebastian looked at his friend and shook his head. He'd asked to be anonymous, claiming he didn't want different treatment from his schoolmates. Really, he was just being a coward again. The next time he'd seen Clay in the halls, he'd been wearing long sleeves, even in the sweltering heat, and had a haunted look. By then, they'd arrested Jesse, and he was going to trial, so the rest of the students gave Clay a wide berth. They ostracized Clay.

He'd been sitting alone at a lunch table when Sebastian had spied him for the first time since the incident. Sebastian had been carrying his lunch tray and detoured by Clay's table. He offered a simple, "How are you doing?"

Clay had warily looked up at him, the ghost of recognition flitting through his eyes. He'd blinked at him, soundlessly picked up his tray still full of food, and tossed it into the closest trash can before leaving the lunchroom.

That was the day Sebastian gathered his emotions, all his secret desires, and locked them up, deep in his soul. If Clay was broken, he had no right to be whole either.

Marc was patting Sebastian's knee and handing him a business card.

"This is completely your decision, Bas. But maybe talking to a professional about this will help you." Sebastian ran his thumb over the embossed cardstock.

"Yeah, maybe." He tucked the card into his wallet. Sebastian stood to get dressed for the rally, unsure how he'd get through the evening. He passed Marc and squeezed his shoulder in passing. "Thank you for listening."

"Any time, bud."

# Chapter 18

## Clay

"I can't believe you won't be here for dinner," Cameron grumbled, sipping her daily allotted eight ounces of coffee, while she glowered from the breakfast nook. Clay huffed and dropped the warm paper bag on the table in front of her. He tossed her the black and white cookie he'd gotten for himself and watched in horror as she tore into the plastic wrap like a feral beast.

"Jesus," he whispered under his breath, "I brought bagels... and trust me, I'd much rather be here." Clay fell into the chair across from her and put his face in his hands. "I have no clue how tonight is going to go."

"If you need me to rescue you, just call. I'll send Colby." Cameron rubbed her giant belly. "Wouldn't want this little one making an early appearance."

"Not much longer now. Only a month left." Clay smiled wistfully, excited to be a new uncle all over again.

"Three weeks and five days… but who's counting?" Cameron shifted and slid out of the chair. "Hang on. Pee break." She passed Colby on her way out of the kitchen. He turned to watch his wife waddle down the hall, hand bracing her back as she groaned.

"Isn't she just beautiful?" Colby sighed longingly and moved to put the defrosted turkey into the finally preheated oven.

"Yeah, she's fine. Just don't go making plans to impregnate my sister again. I very much doubt she wants another one." Clay trudged to the Keurig machine and popped in a pumpkin spice coffee pod.

"No worries on that front. I had a vasectomy months ago," Colby said nonchalantly while he searched the kitchen drawers for the turkey baster. "Such a shame. Cameron is irresistible when she's pregnant with our babies."

Clay made retching noises, eliciting a withering look from Colby, before taking a mug from the coffee bar to finally brew his much needed coffee. As the inky life blood dripped into the mug's hungry maw, Clay tried his best to run scenarios in his head.

Scenario 1: The Riveras figure it out. Bas gets disinherited. No program.

Scenario 2: The Riveras don't figure it out. Bas satisfies Victor's wishes. Program lives. Their "relationship" ends.

Scenario 3: The Riveras don't figure it out. Bas satisfies Victor's wishes. Program lives. Maybe… it doesn't?

Clay smiled despite himself. He finished making his coffee on autopilot while he toyed with the idea of a shirtless Sebastian Rivera in his bed. His dick twitched at the thought. At least he could play out all his fantasies in his head. It was safe there. Clay returned to the table, coffee in hand, and began rustling through the bagels for his cinnamon raisin.

"Why are you smiling like an idiot? Oh my god, you were thinking of him, weren't you?!" Cameron gasped, pulling a sleepy Clarissa by the hand. Charlie slunk in behind them, bleary-eyed. Clay glared at his sister and ignored her question.

"Uncle Clay, are you crushing on someone?" Charlie plopped beside him, mid-yawn, and accepted a warm everything bagel Clay thrust into his hands.

"Like you're one to talk," Clay snorted and ruffled his nephew's new pink hair. Charlie swatted his hand away.

"What can I say? I love love."

Cameron raised an eyebrow at her son while peeling her tired daughter from her side and sliding her onto the bench. Clay's sister tried to silently communicate with him about what Charlie had alluded to, but Clay was suddenly entranced by the cinnamon swirls on his bagel. Charlie's love life was his own. Unless he was in danger, Clay would be sure not to betray his trust.

Clay sighed and slathered his bagel in cream cheese, dreading the next six hours.

Clay rearranged his fake boobs, taking another look at the mirror to ensure his makeup was tasteful and convincing enough. He'd made sure his cheeks were baby smooth and covered with foundation. His brown slouchy sweater allowed him to hide amongst the folds. The jeans were tight, but not uncomfortably so. He was sure his ass looked great. Clay practiced his cockney accent until his phone buzzed.

Sebastian was waiting for him downstairs. Clay took several cleansing breaths, made sure his wig was in place, and clomped out of his apartment in his borrowed ankle boots. If he was being honest, they were a bit too tight. His sister's shoe size was close enough to his that he'd figured he could save Bas the money on footwear. He was regretting his thriftiness when he opened the door to Bas's car and collapsed into the leather seat. He first noticed the delicious smell. Then he noticed Sebastian's unbuttoned collar.

Clay dragged his eyes up to Bas's smirking face. He clearly noticed Clay's appraisal.

"Happy Thanksgiving, Clay."

"Mm, what is that amazing smell?" Clay turned to look in the back seat, spying several bakery boxes.

"Some pies and stuff I baked for dessert." Bas demanded Clay buckle up before pulling away from the curb.

"Boy, you're a baker? Why don't I know this pertinent information?"

"It's just a little hobby. I bake when I'm stressed or frustrated. It's therapeutic." Sebastian shrugged his wide shoulders, palming the wheel as he turned down a side road.

"Been frustrated lately?" Clay said slyly, crossing his legs and leaning back into the seat. Sebastian's grip on the wheel tightened until his knuckles turned white. He cleared his throat and shifted in his seat.

"Maybe," he said, unleashing a hungry look on Clay for the briefest of moments before he turned the car into a long driveway. Clay's heart rattled around in his chest, his face surely flushed. He attempted to get his heart rate under control while simultaneously thanking all the gods for the brief commute. He wasn't sure he'd be able to keep his hands off the hunk of man if he had to spend any more time in an enclosed space with him.

They pulled up to an impressive mini mansion, fully decked out in warm, white Christmas lights. A stray herd of light up reindeer clustered off to the left of the house close to a line of trees. A pearl white nativity scene sat snugly up against the bushes beside the front door. It looked like a goddamn winter wonderland. Clay wondered how much they paid someone to dangle from the roof to string lights across it.

"The fucking Christmas decorations. My god," Bas grumbled as he parked behind a Mercedes.

"Whoa, I didn't expect you to be such a Grinch. You helped *me* decorate my apartment." Clay poked him in the ribs for emphasis. Bas frowned at him, but there was a lightness in his eyes.

"I'm not really. It's just... everything my parents do, it's only for show. Don't get me wrong, they're deeply religious, which is, of course, their prerogative. But all this fanfare? It's as fake as your tits."

Clay gasped and crossed his arms over his padded chest, pulling his British accent out. "Sebastian Rivera! Are you looking at my breasts?"

A thin smile cracked Sebastian's stiff face. Bas did a brief calculation behind his honey eyes before he leaned over the car console and gingerly touched Clay's knee. A zing shot through Clay. *Ohmygod, ohmygod, ohmygod.* He slowly dragged his palm up Clay's leg, stopping just before reaching his crotch. Clay let out a breathy sigh. Sebastian smirked and whispered in his ear, "You know that's not what I'm looking at."

Heat pulsated between them. It was clear to Clay that Sebastian was opening a door. A door that Clay had no business peeking behind... but still. The curiosity was there. If the two remained in their current positions, Clay may kick the goddamn door down. Seeming to sense that, in a rush of cold air, Sebastian was up and out of the car, rounding the hood to open Clay's door. Sebastian looked down at him expectantly before catching sight of the lump in Clay's skinny jeans.

"Oh. I'll give you a minute," he said as he turned to walk away, but Clay's hand shot out to grab his wrist. Stewing in his thoughts would *not* help his situation.

"No, no. I'll be fine. A walk and cold air will help. We're early, right?"

"Yeah. Okay, help me grab a box from the back. We'll take our time going inside."

"Thank you," Clay said with an exhale. Sebastian handed him a box of what he assumed were cookies by the way they clattered around inside. Sebastian balanced the pie boxes in his arms, mule-kicking the door shut behind him. *Yeesh, what a metaphor.* Clay rolled his eyes at his own thoughts and focused on not tripping in his too-tight ankle boots.

Sebastian led the way up to the door, gesturing for Clay to ring the bell. Seconds after pressing the doorbell, a literal butler opened the door. He took the bakery boxes from both of them. Fucking rich people.

"We'll be back, Avery. I want to show Ella the pond." The older gentleman nodded with a stoic smile and turned to bring the boxes further into the house where music and laughter were filtering out. Sebastian quietly closed the door and shoved his hands in his pockets looking down sheepishly at Clay.

"Fuckin' Bruce Wayne motherfucker," Clay scoffed and turned around, stalking around the mini mansion, pretending he knew where he was going. Sebastian quickly reached his side and guided them over to a tree line. A medium-sized man-made pond glittered there in the moonlight. A cacophony of frogs croaked in the brisk air. Bas ducked behind a tree and miniature lanterns winked on, tucked into the branches of the trees overhead.

"Wow," he whispered. Bas took his place beside him, watching as a frog leaped from a stray lily pad.

"You like it?" Bas's gravelly voice was barely above a whisper, his attention on the light reflecting off the pond's surface. Clay looked up at the towering man beside him.

"It's gorgeous."

"This was my happy place when I was a kid." Sebastian briefly clenched his fist before he sighed heavily and looked down at a curious Clay. "I stayed out here all night the day you found Tobias. The day I found you..." Bas squeezed his eyes shut and pinched the bridge of his nose, turning away from him.

"Found me?" Clay stilled, realizing what Bas was saying. Sebastian turned to look into Clay's eyes.

"Yes. It was me." Sebastian's gaze moved back to the pond. "God. There was so much blood." Bas gently reached out and took his wrist. He trailed his thumb over Clay's sleeve, along the scar that snaked up Clay's forearm. Clay's mind was reeling. *Bas? It was Bas who saved me?* He pulled his arm out of his grasp, though not unkindly, and tugged on his sleeves. Sebastian cleared his throat and put his hands back in his pockets. "Well, let's get this night over with."

They turned toward the giant house. Clay took a deep breath, pulled Sebastian's hand from his pocket and laced his fingers through Bas's. Their eyes traveled down to observe their clasped hands.

"Thank you." Clay's voice was quiet, laced with thick emotion. Their eyes met and a tentative smile stretched on Bas's face. He squeezed Clay's hand and tugged him to the front door. Clay's heart galloped. They were at a precipice; he could feel it. They only had to take that next step to tumble forward. But Clay had to keep his feet planted. Nothing good would come from the two of them giving into temptation.

The door opened at Sebastian's knock, but it wasn't Avery, the butler. It was Victor Rivera himself, glass of scotch in hand, cheeks flushed. A sloppy grin appeared on his face as he pulled his son in for a hug. He turned to Clay and put his hand on his shoulder.

"Ella! So glad you could make it. Come on in, you two." He took Clay's coat and immediately handed it to Avery, who had appeared from the shadows. Sebastian handed his coat over to the butler as well, resting his hand on the small of Clay's back. Clay bit the inside of his cheek when he saw Sebastian in the charcoal gray suit with a plum satin button up beneath. *God damn.* They followed Victor into a full room of partially drunk, rich white folk. He introduced Clay to the horde as "Ella, Sebastian's girlfriend." Being from the small town, Clay was surprised he didn't recognize too many faces. He assumed the guests were all from neighboring towns.

Clay waved and made to step into the room, hopefully to disappear into a corner, when Victor held his hand up to halt them. He pointed up above their heads. "Can't enter until you honor the tradition, kids."

Clay wearily glanced above his head to see the flocked ball of mistletoe dangling mere inches from Sebastian's head. Sebastian's eyes quickly made the same journey and landed on Clay. He frowned at his father only to have Victor start a house-wide chant of "Kiss! Kiss! Kiss!" *What a man child.* Clay rolled his eyes at the rest of the group and turned to a glowering Bas. He grabbed Sebastian by his lapels and yanked him down, crushing their lips together.

Sebastian made a surprised grunt while his hands tried to figure out where to put themselves. They landed on his right hip and cupped the back of Clay's head. Sebastian's lips softened and pressed more eagerly into Clay, parting his lips with his tongue. His grip on Clay's hip tightened and pulled him closer against his chest. Clay made a small squeak of surprise at Sebastian's feral reaction. Their tongues tangled a heartbeat too long for a socially acceptable mistletoe kiss.

Sebastian seemed to remember where he was and pulled back with an audible lip-smacking sound. A chorus of hooting and wolf howls echoed around them as they remembered how to breathe again.

"Now, now, son. You're here to eat turkey. Not your girlfriend." Victor chortled, elbowing an older man to his right. Clay and Sebastian laughed weakly. Clay was hoping his sweater was long enough to cover his groin, as there was more blood in his dick than his brain at the moment. Bas closed his hand around Clay's and tugged him through the gaggle of people. Once they'd reached the end of the room and hedged themselves into the kitchen, they sagged against a bare wall.

"I'm sorry. I know how you feel about—"

"It's fine, Bas. Besides, I kissed you."

"Yeah, you have a funny knack of doing that, huh?" Sebastian chuckled low in his throat, his eyes closed. Clay flushed and fussed with his wig as the catering staff milled by, pausing to offer them tequila shots. Bas took two and nodded in thanks, handing one to Clay. They clinked their glasses together and drank their liquid courage. "Alright. Let's go find Mom."

# CHAPTER 19

## Sebastian

Sebastian ran his tongue along his bottom lip, remembering the taste of Clay's mouth. He shook the pestering thoughts from his head and meandered through the kitchen, avoiding the staff with Clay close at his back. Essie was directing the kitchen, true to form. She saw them approaching and turned a kilowatt smile on him.

"*Mijo*," she said quietly while she pulled him into a bear hug. His mother almost never used Spanish, at Victor's insistence. He was mildly stunned to hear her say it in front of a stranger like "Ella" no less.

"Hello Mrs. Rivera. You have a lovely home," Clay said in his cockney accent, offering a hand to her. The two shook and exchanged pleasantries while Sebastian glanced around the kitchen. He spied an idling tray of baby quiches and parked himself in front of it, shoving more than a few in his mouth. He hadn't eaten all day because of nerves.

"Did you get my dessert, Mom?"

"Oh," she uttered, frowning, "yes. I handed them to the caterers." Sebastian caught her obvious discomfort. He gripped the edges of the tray tightly. His parents thought his baking hobby was "too girly." So much so that in middle school, when he'd wanted to join the baking club, his dad had gone over his head and signed him up for debate club instead. So, rather than arguing with Essie, Sebastian popped another quiche into his mouth.

"I can't wait to try them. It smelled heavenly in the car. I can't believe I landed such a stud who also bakes! All my dreams are coming true." Clay slipped to Bas's side and clung to his arm, smiling at him wickedly. A passing look of understanding crossed his face before he turned to Essie. "Oh, Mrs. Rivera, I was wondering, will you be serving any traditional Puerto Rican dishes tonight? I'm excited to try them."

Essie's face tightened. "Oh, I'm sorry, dear. We're having turkey with all the fixings. We usually have Thanksgiving catered."

"No matter, it still smells delicious." Clay beamed, his grip tightening on Sebastian's arm. Sebastian prayed Clay would pull away because his scent was fogging Sebastian's brain. Clay smelled of freshly washed skin and lemon.

*It doesn't smell as delicious as you.*

Clay tipped his head, looking at him in confusion. Sebastian's eyes grew wide. He'd said that out loud. He cleared his throat and stepped back from the redheaded lemon tart clinging to him.

"Come on, Ella. Let's find the bar. I'm parched." Sebastian dragged them away from his gaping mother and quickly found the bar at the far end of the adjoining parlor.

"Hey Bas, you *are* Puerto Rican, right? I hope I didn't offend your mom. She seemed ticked."

"I *am* Puerto Rican. You did nothing wrong. She just feels some kind of way about not being allowed to be authentic." Sebastian ordered two dirty martinis, extra olives, before turning back to Clay.

"Why can't she be authentic?" Clay frowned deeply, putting his hands on his hips. Sebastian's mouth ticked up. This boy was ready to throw down for Essie.

"My dad. He feels it's important for his image to be as white presenting as possible. I never even got to learn Spanish. He banned it in the house." Sebastian scoffed and rolled his eyes. Clay accepted the drink the bartender slid over to them and gingerly pulled Sebastian from the room, away from eavesdroppers. Clay opened a random door, pulling him into the library. He stalked inside, took a deep swig of his martini and turned back to face Sebastian.

"Bas," he said, dropping the accent, "are you serious? Because that's supremely shitty and I may need to punch someone about it."

"Yeah. I'm serious." Clay opened his mouth to protest, but Sebastian held up a hand, silencing him. "I know. He's a controlling bastard. Let's go grab a seat. They should be serving dinner any minute now." Clay frowned at him, unmoving. "Let's just get through tonight, Clay. I'll get my money for your program. Then Ella can conveniently be whisked away to England to care for her ailing aunt or get hit by a bus. Your call." Clay clucked his tongue and led the way out of the library, Sebastian a roiling cloud of grump in his wake.

He figured he'd just drown in alcohol over it. He snaked his way back to the bartender for a knuckle of whisky. Clay nervously hovered around him, nursing his martini as Sebastian quickly finished his glass and held it out for the bartender to refill.

The amber liquid caressed his insides as they mingled with his previous drinks. A sleepy grin appeared on his face, and he slipped an arm around Clay's shoulders as everyone was called to their tables.

His shoulders were so small beneath his arm. Clay had always been a beanpole. Tall, but shorter than Sebastian. The two of them found chairs at the center of the table, because of course.

"Oh, Sebby, we have a special surprise during dessert for you," Essie said, choosing the seats across from them. From his mother's tone, he took it he would not be liking that surprise.

"Oh, goodie," he grumbled as the caterers began serving. Victor stood and drunkenly said grace before the room fell into silence, punctuated by the sound of utensils on ceramic. The food was good as always, but never satisfied Sebastian's appetite for a home cooked meal. Clay was remarkably quiet by his side, focusing his attention on his plate.

He looked nervous. No doubt highly aware of the many eyes on them. Sebastian was more or less used to the gawking, but he understood it could make Clay uncomfortable and that boiled his blood. Sebastian pointedly placed his silverware on the table with a slap and glared daggers at those blatantly staring. They quickly received the message and returned their attention to their dinner.

Clay's hand found his—currently clenched around his fork in a vice grip. He pried the strangled utensil from his fist and threaded their fingers together. Clay squeezed lightly in a quiet thank you. He cleared his throat and looked down the table at Sebastian's parents.

"Mr. and Mrs. Rivera, the food is delicious. Thank you so much for inviting me."

Victor smiled triumphantly and sloppily thundered, "Of course, dear! Say, since you're from across the pond, do you know why Americans celebrate today?"

"Why no, Mr. Rivera. I haven't the foggiest." Clay's voice was filled with an airy wonder, making Sebastian bite down on his lip to keep from grinning. Goddamn, did he love this man. *Wait... love?* Sebastian shook it off, assuming it was the alcohol making him think stupid shit. Sebastian motioned for the waitstaff to continue the flow of whisky. He still wasn't drunk enough to listen to his father.

Meanwhile, Clay was oohing and ahhing as Victor regaled him with the tales of Native American genocide. The other guests listened along, nodding here and there, offering their own anecdotes of history when Victor's words slurred. Clay was still giving an award worthy performance when the doorbell rang. Essie jumped to her feet, a wide grin in place, and excused herself from the table.

*Uh oh.*

"Sebby, could I steal you for a moment," his mother cooed from the adjoining room. Clay's head whipped in his direction, eyes wide. Sebastian smirked and unthreaded their hands, leaning in to kiss him on the cheek.

"Don't worry, I won't leave you to the wolves for long," he whispered in his ear. Sebastian noticed a shiver rake through Clay and his smirk turned wicked. He gently took Clay's chin between his fingers and pressed a pillowy soft kiss against his lips. Clay inhaled sharply as Sebastian quickly slipped away.

In the adjoining room, he found Essie and a stumbling Victor buzzing around a blonde woman. A blonde woman he recognized. He frowned and approached, alcohol thrumming through his blood.

"Miss Whipple. How nice to see you. Happy Thanksgiving," Sebastian said with a grunt. He leveled a glare at Essie, who pretended not to see it.

"Hello, Sebastian." The woman batted her too-long lashes at him. "Wonderful to see you again. You can call me Cassidy." She held her hand out to him in such a way that it seemed she expected him to kiss the back of her hand. He simply took her hand, shook it firmly, and turned to exit the room.

He heard his mother flounder in his wake and ordered a waiter to make Cassidy a plate. Sebastian smiled at his tiny victory, stepping into the kitchen, only to be grabbed around the arm by Victor. His face was mean, all stone and sharp angles.

"How dare you embarrass us like that," he slurred his words, but Sebastian could hear the venom.

"Embarrass you? I'm here with a date and you still invited this woman over to... what? Seduce me? You're trying to pimp me out. It's disgusting." He shook his father off his arm and set about pulling the pies he'd made from their bakery boxes.

"Oh, would you *stop* with the baking shit already?" Victor threw himself onto a stool, clearly intent on harassing his son. Sebastian stilled. He could see the image of Clay in his mind, ready to fight for his honor. Sebastian set the oven to preheat and turned to fully address his father.

"What is your problem with baking?"

"You know what my problem is," Victor hissed, narrowing his eyes. Sebastian scoffed at him.

"Lots of men bake, Dad. Lots of women as well. Not sure if I need to remind you, but it *is* the twenty-first century. Men and women can do the same things."

"Don't sass me! I didn't raise you to be a girl." Something in Sebastian snapped.

"It's measuring shit, mixing it together, and throwing it in an oven! It's not a gendered activity," Sebastian roared. The din from the party quieted and Victor stood from the stool, steel in his gaze. He knocked back the rest of the drink and stared at his son, devoid of warmth.

"You might as well be walking around in heels and a skirt. Because all I see in front of me is a pathetic little bitch of a man." Victor eyed his son up and down. "What a waste of seed."

Victor turned and went to rejoin the party. Sebastian saw red. He made two long strides toward his father, ready to wring his neck, but someone stepped in his way. A hand wrapped around his arm, and yanked him out of the kitchen.

# CHAPTER 20

## Clay

Clay pulled Sebastian through the only door he knew what lay behind it. They were back in the dark library, illuminated only by the bright moon filtering in through the stained-glass window. Clay pushed all six-feet-two inches of Bas into an armchair before truly looking around. Before, he hadn't had the luxury to take in how the light danced rainbows across the endless spines of books.

"Why did you stop me?"

"Bas, do you really want to go to jail?" Clay turned to him. He was clearly drunk. His cheeks were flushed and his head wobbled. The window light bathed him in blues and greens.

"Might as well. Seeing that I'm a 'waste of seed.'"

"Don't listen to him. He's just a bitter old shit who can't stand to see his son excel at things he can't." Clay huffed and sat in the armchair across from him. "You're not the only one with a shitty parent. Turns out there's a lot of them."

"I'm sorry I dragged you into my family drama. We're a mess... *I'm a mess.*" Sebastian sighed and scowled down at the carpeting.

"We're all a little messy sometimes. Don't worry about it... *god, these fucking boots,*" Clay hissed in discomfort and kicked off the ankle boots. His toes throbbed in anguish beneath his socks. He moved to pluck them off, but two large, warm hands encircled his arches.

"Here. Let me." Sebastian sat on the floor and peeled off Clay's socks. Bas pressed his thumbs into the ball of his foot and kneaded. Clay let out a satisfied moan as he massaged his aching feet. Bas paused at the noise, making a little grunt before continuing.

Clay dropped his head back on the chair and bit into his fist. He was hoping not to make any more weird noises. He was always self-conscious about it. It's why he rarely let nail techs massage his feet during a pedicure. But *goddamn,* did that feel good. Another groan escaped him when Bas's fingers found their way to his heel. He could feel the fingers tighten whenever a noise escaped him. *I must be making Bas uncomfortable.*

"I'm sorry for the sounds. I can't help it. My feet are really sensitive." Clay made sure not to look at him for fear of judgment.

"It's fine," he said with a growl. He placed Clay's right foot on his thigh, Bas's rigid length beneath his arch. Electricity ran up Clay's spine. *Holy shit. And Holy. Shit. He* is *big.* Clay swallowed the lump in his throat and hesitantly traced the ridge with his toe. Sebastian made a strangled noise and took Clay's opposite foot in his hands, kneading the flesh. Clay gasped at the sudden touch, pressing the ball of his foot more fully against Bas's arousal.

Bas cursed softly and continued to work the fatigue out of Clay's heel. Feeling his own awakening arousal, Clay let the soft moans fall from his lips, relishing in the way Sebastian's cock twitched beneath his foot each time. By the time Sebastian laid Clay's left foot down, his own erection was straining against his tight jeans. He moved to adjust himself but froze when Sebastian's hands clamped down on his thighs.

They stared at each other in the rainbow light before Clay bit his bottom lip and nodded his agreement. A devastating smile full of want spread across Bas's face as he made quick work of Clay's button and zipper. He yanked the pants down to his ankles, taking in how Clay's cock strained against the fabric of his boxer briefs. Gently, he pulled him free. The touch of Bas's lightly calloused hands made Clay inhale sharply.

Sebastian looked up at Clay, desire darkening his eyes. Slowly, he leaned forward and flicked his tongue against Clay's head, swiping away the bead of precum. Lightning bolts ping-ponged through his nervous system as Sebastian took another exploratory lick.

"*Fuck, Bas*," Clay groaned and sunk his fingers into Sebastian's silky hair. Bas chuckled and nuzzled his base.

"Clay, fair warning. I haven't done this much, so I'm not sure if I'll be that good." He circled his thumb around the head, making Clay curse again.

"Trust me, you can't do it wrong. But, Bas," Clay tilted Sebastian's chin up to look at him. "It doesn't matter. I want you. It wouldn't matter if you were the most experienced gay who ever existed or a virgin." Clay cupped Sebastian's cheek and Bas pressed back, a heart-breaking smile on his lips.

"Just for that, I'm going to make sure I suck the soul out of your dick."

Clay snorted a surprised laugh that quickly turned into a gasp for air when the full length of Bas's tongue traced his shaft. When Sebastian took him in his hot mouth, Clay almost fainted. He'd been fantasizing about being sucked off by Sebastian Rivera for longer than he liked to admit. Having it happen was surreal, to say the least. And regardless of what Sebastian had said about his inexperience, Clay was sinking his nails deep into the leather of the armchair with each pull of Sebastian's lips.

Clay dropped his head back and secured his arm over his mouth to muffle his guttural moans. Sebastian hummed a deep laugh, which deliciously vibrated through Clay's cock.

"Don't worry. Library is soundproof," Bas said, pulling his mouth away briefly, pumping Clay with his hand. Clay removed his arm and hissed his pleasure before locking his eyes with Sebastian again. He was rewarded with a smile. "Good boy. Eyes on me." Then he plunged his mouth down Clay's throbbing length.

Clay groaned loudly and fisted his hand in Sebastian's hair, jerking against him. Sebastian hummed another chuckle and sucked more voraciously, hollowing his cheeks. Clay gasped and pulled Sebastian off him, worried he'd bust too soon.

"Wait. I want to see you," Clay panted, pointing down to the hard lump in Sebastian's pants. Sebastian growled and nuzzled against Clay's wet shaft before he pulled back, standing so he could remove his belt. Clay used his own hand to pump himself while his eyes devoured Sebastian's slow, deliberate stripping. First, the belt dropped into a coil on the wood floor. Then he pried his button up open, exposing the taught muscles of his chest and abs. Clay purred in the back of his throat, dangerously close to the edge.

Sebastian unzipped his slacks, leaving his Adonis belt on full display. Bas watched as Clay masturbated for a moment before slipping his hand into his waistband, grunting as he wrapped his hand around his shaft. When he pulled himself free, Clay paused in his pumping, content to watch as Sebastian slid his hand up and down his own cock. Clay's throat bobbed in response.

"C'mere. And don't stop on my account," Clay said, voice rough with want. Sebastian barked a laugh and fell to his knees, still pleasuring himself. He settled between Clay's legs and kissed his cockhead before swallowing him whole. "*Fuuuuuuck,*" Clay groaned, cupping the back of Sebastian's head. He was buried so deep in Bas's throat he nearly tumbled off the edge of bliss right then. Clay could barely keep the impending orgasm at bay, thinking of anything *but* the way Sebastian greedily sucked him.

"Bas... I'm close." Clay shifted to pull out, but Sebastian pinned him against the chair, his hand splayed across Clay's chest. Sebastian sucked even harder, his own jerking becoming erratic. Clay melted back into the chair and used both of his hands to secure Bas's head, bucking into his mouth. The two moaned in unison as Clay fucked Sebastian's mouth.

Seconds later, stars exploded behind Clay's eyes as he came in the back of Sebastian Rivera's throat. He jerked against him roughly, eliciting a wild shout from Sebastian as he came with him. Sebastian extracted himself from Clay's cock, keeping his gaze as he swallowed.

"*Jesus,*" Clay muttered. He was boneless and more satisfied than he'd been in a long time. A lazy smile snaked on his face as he looked at the delicious man before him.

Then he heard a door click shut.

Clay shot up in a panic. Had someone seen them?

"Did you hear that?" Clay's voice was barely above a whisper.

"It's fine, Clay. No one comes in here." Sebastian crawled up to Clay and pressed a kiss to his lips. "God, I really want to do that again."

Clay smiled, trying to keep the worry from his face. Sebastian was too booze drunk or too sex drunk to notice. He kissed him once more before straightening to button his shirt. Clay quickly shimmied his jeans back into place, pulled his socks on, and slid back into the demon booties. Clay jogged—painfully—to the door.

"Clay?"

"I figure we shouldn't be seen leaving the same room," he threw false cheer into his words, silently freaking out as he straightened his wig and clothes. He didn't want his horniness to ruin the entire plan.

"Who cares? We're adults, not teenagers."

"True. But do you really want to give your dad anything else to hold over your head?" Sebastian was silent behind him. Clay felt slimy for manipulating him. When a response didn't come, Clay cleared his throat. "Okay, I'll go first."

He slipped out of the library, quietly shutting the door behind him. He strode through the hall chanting in his mind, *remember to be British, remember to be British.*

"Are you done corrupting my son?" A gruff voice rumbled out from the door Clay had just passed. He skidded to a halt and turned to face Victor Rivera.

"Ello, Mr. Rivera. You quite startled me," Clay poured on the accent a smidge too thickly.

"You can drop the act," Victor said, scowl fixed in place. He stepped forward, another drink in his hand. He wobbled a bit but had enough of his wits to stay upright. "I don't know what escort service Sebastian hired you from, but I'll double your pay to never speak to him again." Clay frowned, crossing his arms.

"Excuse me, sir. Did you ever stop to think that I may actually love your son?" *Holy shit, what?!*

"Please. I know how cold he is. No one could love that idiot." He rummaged around in his pocket and produced two crumpled hundreds. He tossed them in Clay's direction. "Take that for now. I'll send a more formal payment next week."

"I don't want your money." Venom dripped from Clay's voice. He was barely clinging to the accent.

Victor stilled and narrowed his eyes. He shuffled into Clay's face, hate shining in his eyes. "Get out of my house, *boy*," he spat, shoving past Clay to return to the festivities. Ice ran through his veins. *Victor knows.* Clay ground his teeth and eyed the money on the floor. He snatched it up, intending to donate it. Better for it to be in the hands of the needy than that prick.

Clay knew he couldn't stay, not after Victor confronted him. The man could turn his poison on Sebastian and Clay would very much like to not be jailed for assault. With a deep sigh, he texted Sebastian that he had an emergency and ran for the door before he could second guess himself.

# CHAPTER 21

## Zamboni

The man in the hood smelled wrong.

Zamboni sniffed the air, his hackles rising. Krystal was speaking with another human woman, unaware of Zamboni's concern. Usually, he'd be hunting the chipmunks down. They'd relocated their main den since he'd broken into the last one. But in the presence of the hooded man, the chipmunks were forgotten.

He sat at his master's side, unwilling to stray from her. Zamboni was wary of the man who was observing the space on the town hall wall that was littered with papers. It was where Krystal had shown him a picture of a very nice-looking dog and pasted it near some other papers. Zamboni thought he recognized the images of the men who sat beside the picture of the dog but entirely disregarded the thought when Hood Man started ripping little bits off the papers.

"Zambo, what are you doing over here? Go run around!" Krystal pet Zamboni's head and gestured to the park with her hand. He lolled his tongue vacantly and stood, trotting closer to the man. As long as he could keep the hooded man in his sight and away from Krystal, he'd do as she expected.

He slipped behind a bush, out of Krystal's sight, and could see Hood Man more clearly. He peeled pre-cut rectangles from the bottoms of some papers and shoved them into his pocket. Hood Man paused as he stepped up to the papers of the dog and the men. His hand traced over both pictures of the men before violently ripping the papers down. Hood Man growled and punched the wall where the papers danced in tatters.

Zamboni stepped forward, a growl low in his throat. This man was dangerous, and he wouldn't allow him near his master. Or even the chipmunks, for that matter. Hood Man looked over his shoulder at Zamboni's warning. He bared his fangs for emphasis. The man huffed and walked off just as Krystal called Zamboni back to her side.

# CHAPTER 22

## Sebastian

Sebastian had an excess of lemon bars in his fridge. So many that he had nowhere to put the new batch in his hands. He growled in frustration and slammed the tray down on the kitchen counter, causing a few squares to dislodge from the others.

Since Thanksgiving, Clay had gone radio silent... again. Besides the cryptic text, Sebastian had no idea if he'd scared him off. Was the blow job *that bad*? He seemed to like it. Clay's lemon scent had haunted him since, hence, the excess of lemon-flavored pastries scattered around his kitchen.

His phone angrily buzzed from beneath an empty flour bag, jerking him out of his fit of anger. He answered the phone with a growly, "What?"

"Sebastian," his father's disapproving voice chirped in his ear.

"Sorry, Dad. What's up?" He hadn't spoken to Victor since he'd called the day after Thanksgiving. He'd been blackout drunk and called to apologize, which was shocking. Victor remembered nothing but heard from Essie that Ella left abruptly after he'd spoken to her. It was clear his father was to thank for Clay's avoidance.

"I snagged you a meeting with Stella Simmons in approximately—" he heard paper rustling on the opposite end, "—thirty minutes."

"Dad! It takes almost twenty minutes to drive there. You couldn't give me more notice?" Sebastian aggressively wrapped tinfoil over the squares and rushed around, looking for his loafers.

"This was all the time she had available for months. Make sure to win her back to our side. If we can help boost their sales, the taxes alone will be worth the effort.."

Sebastian cursed, tripping over his rug while tossing his apron onto the counter. Grabbing a clip-on tie, which he rarely used, he ended the call with his father and grabbed his keys on the way out of the door.

"And why should I back you, Mr. Rivera? Mr. Emmerson has already assisted our business enormously with his advertising know-how." Stella Simmons arched a dark brow, the irritation clear on her face.

"I agree. The help from Cl— Mr. Emmerson was a step in the right direction. But to think about future improvements, not to mention possible expansion, you'll need more liquidity. The more the casino makes, the better Wellsprings' economy will be."

Sebastian had a fake smile plastered on his face, hands steepled on the conference table. There was a twist in his gut from betraying Clay like this. Although the fiery redhead had made it abundantly clear that he wouldn't stop fighting for the election regardless of their agreement. Sebastian would be doing him a disservice if he yielded. Stella pursed her lips, expecting him to continue.

"I'm sure I could convince my father's developmental team to help assist in any plans you might have for the casino at a discounted rate. If I recall, you had been looking to add a concert hall to compete with the big boys."

Stella's eyes widened, and she shifted uncomfortably in her chair. *Gotcha.*

"Yes, my team has been discussing the possibility. Funding hasn't been as easy to come by. Although revenue has certainly increased in the past months, to take on a job of this size requires... more." She leaned forward in her chair. "I won't lie to you, Mr. Rivera. You offer a sweet deal. But what would this mean for Clay's campaign? He's a nice boy and has done so much for this community. I'm not sure I could live with myself if my decision cost him the election."

Sebastian's smile faltered. Whatever Stella saw swirling in Sebastian's gaze made her smile coyly. "You want him to win. Don't you?"

"Wh—no, of course not. I've worked very hard to get where I am and truly want to improve Wellsprings. Mr. Emmerson is also a competent candidate, and I don't doubt that if he were to be elected, he too would better the town. I just believe in my vision more."

"And what vision is that exactly?" Stella held up a hand as Sebastian rattled off his campaign notes. "No. Tell me where *your* ideal place to live is."

"I... well, where everyone knows your name. Where people don't have to worry about being judged." Sebastian's fist tightened on the table. "Where you can be yourself. A society that comes together in the face of tragedy." Sebastian's gut twisted as he thought of Tobias. Almost half of the town had skipped the candlelight vigil once they discovered Tobias had been homosexual. "To love one another. Regardless of politics, status, or sexuality."

Stella's hand reached across the table and patted his still clenched fist.

"That sounds like a wonderful place."

Sebastian fiddled with the now pliable business card in his palm. He'd been carrying it in his pocket since Marc gave it to him. The edges were all worn out from playing with it in the waiting room. After his heart-to-heart, with Stella Simmons of all people, he figured it was time to make the call.

He had a feeling that if he wanted to live in a town full of love and acceptance, he should start with himself. Doctor Ambrose, one of only three therapists in Wellsprings, had happily squeezed him into his schedule. But then again, Doctor Ambrose was thrilled to treat anyone whose name he could drop at parties. Sebastian wasn't exactly sure if that was a HIPPA violation or not, but he was the only doctor who could squeeze him in at such short notice.

If Sebastian started therapy and worked on himself, then maybe he'd be brave enough to seek Clay. Find out what had driven him away. Sure, technically the terms of their agreement were fulfilled, but didn't Clay know Sebastian was serious about him? They couldn't just ignore the chemistry between them.

After the election, there would be no excuse. Sebastian wouldn't let the chance slip past him again. He smiled to himself and wondered what high school Sebastian would say about their little entanglement now.

"Thank you again for seeing me, Doctor Ambrose." A quiet voice drifted in the air. Sebastian's head snapped up. He knew that voice.

Clay stepped into the waiting room, shouldering on a windbreaker. He skidded to a halt when he caught Sebastian's gaze. Clay's cheeks immediately flooded with pink as he locked his eyes on the exit ahead.

Sebastian shot up from his chair and stalked over to him, voice a low grumble, "Why have you been ghosting me?"

Clay crossed his arms instead of answering the question. "Why are you here?"

"Self-improvement and all that. Clay, what happened on Thanksgiving?" Sebastian gripped Clay's bicep. Clay's eyes slid to where they were in contact and looked back sharply.

"Nothing. Our deal is done, isn't it?"

"You sent me a text saying there was an emergency."

"It was a personal emergency. I don't need to explain myself to you."

Sebastian sighed and released his hold on Clay's arm. "No, you absolutely don't. I was just worried. I thought maybe... you didn't like what happened. I wanted to apologize." Sebastian rubbed the back of his neck in embarrassment and Clay's face twisted in pain.

"No... Bas. What happened in the library was great. But as fun as it was, we can't let it happen again. Things are too messy." Clay shook his head and edged toward the door. The receptionist—who had been not so discreetly watching their interaction—called Sebastian's name to tell him the doctor was ready for him.

Sebastian frowned and Clay sighed, patting his shoulder. "Just let it go," he said before slipping out the door.

# CHAPTER 23

## Clay

Seeing Sebastian in the lobby of a therapist's office made Clay's dick hard as granite. He cursed to himself in a steady stream as he took the stairs two at a time. The more distance he put between himself and Sebastian Rivera, the safer his heart would be.

Clay paused in the stairwell to answer the phone bleating in his pocket. He'd missed a few calls from Tanya during his session, so it must have been urgent.

"Hey Tanya, sorry I was in a meeting."

"Clay. Stella Simmons called. The casino is pulling their support. Rivera stole them out from under us."

"Sebastian?! What... how?" To think that smarmy bitch had tried to cozy up to him mere moments ago. Without the casino publicly backing him, Clay's campaign was as good as dead in the water. The townsfolk of Wellsprings looked to the casino as a financial god. If the casino flourished, so did the town. "Did she say why?"

"Rivera offered her a development deal. I have to admit it's a good deal, and it was probably the only hand he had to play."

"Crap. Well, how badly will that set us back?" Clay grumbled a curse and scrubbed his face. With the money coming from Sebastian for the bullying program, that gave him some room to play with the town budget. He knew he shouldn't bank on Sebastian's word alone, but if he was going to make a difference in Wellsprings, he'd need to get elected first. Tanya shuffled papers in the background, pulling him back from his inner spiral.

"Based on the questionnaires we sent out, the casino's prosperity comes second to only one thing. The conservation of the Palmer chipmunk."

"You're kidding me. The chipmunks are what everyone cares about?"

"Well, they *are* endangered. Ever since they were identified, we've had conservationists begging to come in and relocate them. But, since they're thriving here, they've been unsure if they *should* move them."

"Hang on, didn't the Husky breach their den? I swear I saw a video."

"Yes. My friend sent it to me. I'll send it to you."

The ping of a received message chimed in Clay's ears seconds later. Tanya was nothing if not efficient. Clay flipped the phone around and watched the video of Mayoral Candidate Zamboni chasing the chipmunks through the town square garden.

"If he did it once, maybe he can do it again. Tanya, can you get one of the conservationists' numbers?"

"You got it, boss."

Clay collapsed on a bench outside the high school. He'd promised to pick up Charlie from school today while Cameron and Colby were at a sonogram appointment. Clarissa's daycare was his next stop. Clay shuddered a sigh and dragged a tired hand through his ginger hair. He'd been on several phone calls since leaving the therapist's office that morning. He'd need to drop into his campaign office at some point that evening to go over the new direction they'd be taking.

More importantly, he and his crew would need to go over his next speech for the debate at the end of the week. He'd have to see Sebastian again. He'd have to argue with him... professionally. After their hesitant friendship, Clay wasn't sure if he could remain impartial anymore. He wasn't sure when it happened, but somewhere along the way, he'd started to fall. But he couldn't. He swore to himself he'd never love another man again. Not since Toby. Not since Clay survived. He didn't deserve it.

Clay shook himself out of his funk just as the school bell rang. He wearily rose from his bench, melding into the throng of waiting parents and guardians. Kids erupted from the doors moments later, breaking into their separate cliques. The mass of parents dwindled as they received their respective wards. Clay nervously stood on his tip-toes. He rarely picked up his nephew and was concerned he'd missed him somehow.

Wellsprings was by no way a large town, so it could've been possible Charlie decided to walk home. He was about to pull out his phone and call when a shock of pink hair caught his eye. Charlie was beside a sandy-haired boy in a heated discussion. Clay frowned, ready to go bitch out a teenager when he saw Charlie grasp the boy's arms rather desperately. The boy shrugged him off, a look of pain on his face.

"Brennan!" A shout came from Clay's right. Something about the deep baritone made a trickle of fear drip down Clay's spine. He knew that voice. It was deeper than remembered, but he could almost hear the echoing words of hate. Clay didn't move, eyes still trained on Charlie and his friend. The sandy-haired boy jerked his head toward the voice. Charlie reached a hand toward the boy, Brennan, but hesitated when Brennan shot a glare at him over his shoulder. Charlie dropped his hand, and Brennan stalked off. Clay swallowed a thick lump in his throat and slowly turned to find the owner of the voice.

Jesse Manella's black-brown eyes bore into him, an amused half smirk slashed across his face. His jaw was squarer than Clay remembered, with a noticeable scar sliced through his right eyebrow. Brennan's arrival diverted Jesse's attention, completely ignoring Clay's existence as he roughly turned Brennan around and walked away.

"Uncle Clay?" His nephew's concerned voice was at his side. Clay hadn't taken his eyes off Jesse's back.

"That boy, Brennan. He's the one you like?" Clay's tone was eerily calm.

"Yeah," Charlie admitted in a resigned huff. "But he's been so cold to me since his uncle moved in."

Clay's eyes shot back to Charlie. His nephew took a hesitant step back from his intense stare. Clay took several calming breaths before placing his hands on Charlie's shoulders.

"Charlie. I know you like him, and things are tough right now. But stay far away from him. Especially his uncle."

Charlie nodded, clearly unsure why Clay was reacting this way, but understanding eventually widened his eyes.

"Is he—"

"Yes," Clay barked. He looped an arm around his nephew's shoulders and pulled him down the block in the opposite direction of his old high school tormentor.

Clay kept himself together all the way to Cameron's house, Clarissa and Charlie in tow. Once he got the kids settled with snacks (pizza rolls for Charlie and goldfish for Clarissa), he made Charlie vow to watch his sister like a hawk. He was too close to having a nervous breakdown and had to get out of there.

He found himself where he always did whenever the icy fangs of panic lodged themselves in his spine—Wellsprings Cemetery. Clay stared down at the headstone. A light coat of moss had filmed over the top since he'd last visited. A cluster of sunflowers rested at the base, the petals starting to brown. Clay was sure they were from Toby's mother. He usually saw her around town, purchasing sunflowers every Sunday. Sunflowers were Toby's favorite. Once he was elected, he would have to remember to plant some sunflowers in the town square gardens.

Clay released a long sigh and sank onto the cold ground. He pulled out the bag of Dipsy Doodles, Toby's favorite snack, popping the bag open. The salty corn chip smell immediately assaulted his senses. Clay had never been a fan of corn chips of any kind, but whenever he visited with Toby, he would suddenly find himself able to stomach them. In a weird way, it made him feel like Toby was near.

"Hey Toby. Sorry, it's been a minute since I've visited." The slight stirring of crisp autumn leaves was his only response. A single bright red leaf drifted down and gracefully landed on Clay's thigh. He picked it up by the stem, slowly twirling it in his fingers.

"A lot has been going on." His mind strayed to Bas, immediately feeling guilty. "Do you remember Sebastian Rivera? Hunky football star from high school? Well, turns out he plays for team rainbow. And I think he likes me... which is crazy. But he *did* give me a blow job and all." Clay felt his cheeks heat and immediately crunched on a doodle, feeling a bit silly for being embarrassed when he only spoke to the empty air.

"So... funny thing is, I think I like him back. Like a lot... Shit, am I in love with that bastard?" Clay raked his fingers through his hair in distress. "Well anyway. Things are a mess right now. And fucking Jesse is back." Clay curled his legs up and wrapped his arms around them, burying his face in his knees. "I'm so scared Toby. When I saw him, all I could think was how I'd been too weak to stop the bullying. I couldn't protect you... and then I was stupid enough to try to join you. I knew you'd hate me for it. But it just hurt so much."

A strangled sob choked him, cutting off his words. He quietly cried while the autumn breeze tousled his hair in a gentle caress. Once his eyes were puffy and red, he unfurled himself once more, drowning his pain in the Dipsy Doodles.

"Bas found me. It was him who saved me," Clay said in barely a whisper. "I want to give him a chance, but I don't know if I can let you go." Clay looked up from the ground and froze, his breath catching in his throat. Sitting on top of Tobias's gravestone was a bright red cardinal. The small bird tilted his head, regarding Clay's stunned expression. The bird didn't flinch or shuffle about anxiously. It simply watched him.

Tears blurred the edges of his vision again. He tentatively reached a hand toward the bird, its head jerked up, the crown of feathers shooting up in warning. Clay snatched his hand back, afraid he might scare it away. His voice was thick with emotion when he spoke.

"Is it okay? For me to move on?"

Clay absently pulled a doodle from the bag and the cardinal hopped off the gravestone and onto his knee. The bird pointedly looked at the chip in his hand. Ever so slowly, Clay extended the chip to the bird. The cardinal hopped closer to his approaching hand, accepting the doodle once it was within beak's reach.

Clay watched in wonder as the little bird balanced on his leg and nibbled on the chip, glancing up at him periodically. It finished the doodle, shook out its feathers, and hopped back up to Clay's knee. It made a little chirp, giving Clay one long lingering look before it flew into the brisk sunset.

# CHAPTER 24

## Sebastian

The trees had all dropped their foliage.

Crisp leaves crumbled under Sebastian's boot as he trudged through the crowd behind Victor. Sebastian had never seen so many pride flags at a political rally before. Stepping to his father's side, Sebastian jammed his hands into his jean's pockets, glowering up at the podium. Clay's name glared back at him from several banners and posters amidst random Christmas decor that had no business being at a mayoral rally. Since he'd bumped into him at the therapist's office two weeks ago, Sebastian hadn't heard from him. Then again... it's not like he'd reached out either.

When the Emerson campaign had leaked that a special announcement would be made at the next rally, Victor advised they should attend to see just exactly what they were going to have to maneuver. Sebastian eagerly agreed. Even if Clay didn't speak to him, at least he'd be out of the house, not baking more of the lemony treats that'd quickly taken up all the flat surfaces in his apartment.

A chorus of claps roared from the crowd when Clay approached the podium. Sebastian's heart lodged in his throat when Clay's red hair came into view. He'd grown a beard since he'd last seen him. It was tapered expertly and did wonders for his jawline. *Holy fuck.*

Clay addressed the crowd warmly, fielding some basic questions right off the bat regarding the loss of the casino's support.

"I'm grateful to the Rivera team. They were able to promise to help improve and expand the casino where I wasn't. And while we're on the subject of change, I'd like to bring to you my new plan for Wellsprings."

The crowd fell into silence. Waiting with bated breath. If Sebastian was being honest, so was he. Clay was captivating when he was in the zone. Sebastian chewed on his lip and shook his head free of the lewd thoughts unjustly parading in his mind, which mainly featured Clay bent over the podium. God, he needed to get laid. No doubt, he'd be baking his sexual frustration away tonight as well.

"What makes our great town stand out on the map? Is it the casino? Is it the stunning views of the mountains? It should be, but it isn't. No, the Palmer chipmunk is what Wellsprings is known for."

Murmurs went up in the audience. Faintly, Sebastian heard his father say, "Well shit."

Clay laid out his plans with the conservationist groups. He was thorough. So much work had been done in mere weeks. *He deserves this. Not me.* Sebastian had half a mind to stomp up to the podium himself and revoke his candidacy. He looked at his father, who wore a deep scowl on his tanned face.

One year.

Nine months and sixteen days, to be precise.

Then Sebastian's trust would be all his. It figured that the controlling Victor Rivera would place an age restriction of thirty-six on the assets. Sebastian folded his arms, turning his angry glare fully on the back of his father's head. He only had to make it till September. Then his dad could fuck right off. Sure, winning the vote would make his relationship with Victor easier until then, but Sebastian never wanted to be mayor. Clay deserved it.

"I have to give a big shout out to the mayoral candidate, Zamboni. Without him, we may have never discovered a way to find the chipmunks' dens." The goofy, Husky candidate pranced onto the stage, tongue lolling, his owner close behind, holding the lead in a death grip. The crowd went insane. Chipmunks, a derpy dog, and a proud gay on stage? Sebastian knew one thing. He wasn't going to win. He grinned.

Sebastian's wild smile caught Clay's gaze. He'd gone stock still on the stage as the crowd hooted around them. Sebastian's smile turned wicked, and he winked at Clay before turning to find his way home.

To bake a fucking lemon pie.

Two weeks later, Sebastian found himself drinking whisky heavily in front of his parents' raging fireplace. It was Christmas Eve, the one night when his father wasn't hobnobbing with the rich. Victor sat in a plush armchair beside him, reading some book on politicking. Sebastian rolled his eyes and looked back at the crackling fire instead.

"Sebby! Come help me a moment in the kitchen," Essie hollered. Sebastian downed the rest of his drink and dutifully went in search of his mother. Essie rarely cooked traditional Puerto Rican dishes. Christmas Eve was the one day a year the Rivera household wasn't hosting an extravagant party. As such, Victor allowed Essie to make whatever she liked.

A muscle ticked in Sebastian's jaw at the reminder of how Victor had erased their culture. The savory, garlicky scent of the *pernil al horno* wrapped him in a hug as he entered the kitchen. His mother was making flan and mixing cookie dough at the same time, sweat glistening on her brow.

"Oh, good! Can you add some water to the pork pan? Dinner should be ready soon."

"Sure, Mom." He opened the oven, inhaling deeply. "It smells delicious." He added the water and plopped himself at the kitchen island, taking the bowl of cookie dough from her. "I can help." Essie smiled and nodded at him, taking the flan to the fridge to set. "I love your cooking."

"Thank you, sweetheart."

Sebastian mixed the sticky dough, his irritation rising. "It's a shame you're not allowed to cook more often."

Essie froze, half in the refrigerator. "Yes, well... we're always so busy."

Sebastian slammed the bowl down on the counter, the whiskey loosening his tongue. "Cut the bullshit, Mom. You know it's because of *him*."

"*Mijo*! Lower your voice." Essie glared at him, slamming the fridge shut behind her. "You will not ruin this evening. I will not argue about this *again*."

"How can you just go along with everything he says? Don't you have any self-respect?"

"Sebastian! I've told you. It's for the good of our family. I stand by my husband, in all things."

Sebastian ground his teeth together, gripping the edge of the counter. "*All* things? Even when it comes to me?"

"What are you talking about?" Essie snatched the bowl from his grasp, wrapping the top with plastic wrap. Victor had edged himself into the room, the book he'd been reading tucked under his arm. Sebastian glowered at his father before turning back to Essie.

"Do you remember when I was in college? I asked you and Dad to dinner because I wanted to tell you something."

"Oh! Yes. Something about your roommate. You two had grown close, was it?" The blank look on his mother's face enraged him.

"He was my boyfriend."

Victor scoffed at his right, dropping the book on the counter with more force than necessary.

"For what? Three months? Then you graduated and never spoke to him again." Victor grunted and searched a cabinet for a glass.

"Young people do a lot of experimenting in college. It was just a little fling," Essie said, gently pushing Victor to the side to yank a glass from the shelf and place it in his palm.

"No. No, it wasn't. I'm gay. I told you then and I'm telling you now." Sebastian's heart cracked a little in his chest.

"No," Victor said simply, pouring himself two fingers of scotch.

"No? You can't tell me 'no.' It isn't a question!" Sebastian's fists balled together at his side.

"I say no, because you have clearly forgotten about your girlfriend, Ella." Victor raised a skeptical eyebrow at him, looking at his wife as if their son was certifiably insane.

"You know Ella isn't a woman. His acting isn't *that* good."

"What?" Essie's pupils widened in shock. *Okay, maybe it was that good.*

"That's enough. We're not discussing this any further." Victor turned on his heel and walked back out to the living room. Sebastian stared across the island at his mother. Her face contorted into a pained expression.

"You stand with your husband? You'll deny my feelings?" Sebastian stood, bracing his hands on the counter, waiting for the inevitable blow. Essie's lip quivered, emotions warring behind her eyes until a rattling sigh escaped her. She cast her eyes downward, abashedly hanging her head.

His heart shattered.

He had to swallow the lump in his throat before speaking. "You shame me, your heritage, but most importantly, you shame yourself." Sebastian turned his back to her and walked straight out the door. He stomped down the walkway, abandoning his car. He'd been drinking and knew he shouldn't be driving. Tears streamed down his cheeks, the cold air quickly robbing them of heat.

He walked the quiet streets of Wellsprings, families tucked in their homes to celebrate. Families who loved each other. Sebastian thought of his empty apartment, filled with lemony confections and loneliness. He wasn't sure he could bring himself to stew in his depression there. There was only one person he needed at that moment. Sebastian pulled his phone from his pocket and dialed before he lost courage.

It rang twice before a raucous noise erupted from the receiver. A little girl's peeling laughter, Christmas music on blast, and a distressed Clay shouting that he was excusing himself for a moment. A warbled smile found its way onto Sebastian's face. The noise died down with the sound of a closing door.

"Hello? Shit, it's cold out here."

"Clay?" Sebastian tried to keep the emotion out of his voice, but he doubted it was convincing enough.

"Bas? What's wrong?"

"I told them. I told them and they dismissed me. Again. On fucking Christmas Eve," his voice cracked with emotion. He ran a palm down his face, composing himself before continuing. "I don't know why I thought it would be different. But I left. I was so mad. So disappointed. Why can't my family love me like yours does?" The tears were falling freely now.

"Where are you?"

"Outside."

"Bas, work with me here. What street are you on?"

Sebastian had to wipe away the tears to see the closest street sign.

"Corner of Rosewater and Chestnut."

There were little pants coming from the receiver now. Was he running? A gust of cold hit the back of his neck. Sebastian glanced up at the sky to see a delicate flurry of snowflakes fluttering around him and peppering his hair. He could hear feet slapping the pavement now.

"Bas? Turn around."

He turned to see a frazzled Clay sprinting toward him, phone still plastered to his ear. He skidded to a halt, gasping for air. His cheeks were flushed, a scarf haphazardly thrown around his neck, hair wild, and he'd never looked more beautiful.

"Hi," Sebastian said into the phone.

"Hi," Clay said back, ending the call and shoving his phone into his back pocket. He quickly closed the distance and pulled Sebastian into a tight hug.

Sebastian wrapped his arm around Clay's shoulder, burying his other hand in Clay's hair. He held him tight, dropping his forehead onto Clay's shoulder, letting the last of the tears leak out silently. His sweet lemony scent wrapped around him.

"Ahhh, you're warm," Clay grumbled, trying to snuggle closer. Sebastian chuckled weakly.

"You're not wearing a jacket? What's wrong with you?" He disentangled himself from Clay and shrugged off his coat.

"I rushed out to hug a distressed fellow gay. Wait, don't give me your coat!"

"Shut up. I have a sweater on, I'm fine," he said gruffly, draping the coat around Clay's shoulders. Snowflakes danced around them, glistening on Clay's rosy cheeks. Sebastian smiled despite himself and cupped Clay's face, wiping the melting flakes away with a brush of his thumbs. "Thank you for coming."

Clay's green eyes sparkled in the light of nearby Christmas decorations. A hand fisted Sebastian's sweater for a moment, then trailed down his arm to twine their fingers together. His breath caught. *Is he going to kiss me?* Clay finally smiled softly and pushed away from Sebastian.

"Come with me."

# Chapter 25

## Clay

In the past, Clay would've balked at bringing home a guy for Christmas. He'd never introduced any man to his sister, apart from Toby. Now he stood in the foyer, hand in hand with his political rival, dusting snowflakes from his hair.

Clarissa ran up to them immediately, eagerly squealing, catching the attention of his sister. She gaped at the pair of them, eyes sparkling with mischief.

"Santa's coming!" Clarissa's eyes were unhinged. She must have been on her tenth cookie, the sugar high still going strong. Clay nodded and pulled off his coat—Bas's coat—hanging it on the hook. He was about to step around his niece to introduce his tag-along when Clarissa threw up her hands.

"Mistletoe!" she shrieked in a sugar-induced glee. Clay looked up at the meddlesome decoration, cursed, and looked over his shoulder at Bas, who had a suspiciously devilish gleam in his eye.

"This keeps happening to us," he said in a deep whisper.

"I'm sorry, just ignore her. She has a sugar problem," he stage-whispered, trying to get around her.

"No! Kiss! It's the rules!" Clarissa made a pouty face.

"Far be it from me to deny a child's wishes on Christmas Eve," Bas said, yanking Clay against his chest. "You game?"

Clay flushed. He nodded and wrapped his arms around Bas's neck, comfortable in the safety of his family. Bas planted his hands on Clay's waist and took his mouth in a gentle caress. His tongue flicked against his lip, and Clay eagerly opened his mouth for him. Their tongues slid against each other. Once, twice, then Bas respectfully pulled back.

Clay smiled stupidly at him, alarmed when someone cleared their throat. He glanced over to see the entire family standing in the hallway wearing matching grins. Charlie hooted until his father flicked him in the back of the head. Bas sheepishly introduced himself, placing his hand on the small of Clay's back. Electricity raced up Clay's spine from the touch. *Well, this is going to be interesting.*

Charlie kept staring at Bas, then at his uncle, then back again. "I can't believe it," he finally said. "You don't present as gay at all. I have great gaydar."

"That's what I said!" Cameron slapped her hand against the table as Colby served steak and mashed potatoes.

"First of all! Offensive language. Sexuality does not always reflect in personalities." Clay leveled a half-hearted glare at the pair. Charlie raised his hands in surrender.

"You're right. I guess that's kind of Brennan's deal." Charlie scooped a hearty helping of potatoes onto his plate. Clay stiffened.

"You're not still seeing him, are you?" The question rang in the sudden quiet. Cameron raised her eyebrows and looked back at her son with worry.

"Not since you told me about his Uncle Jesse. I listen when you talk." Charlie rolled his eyes and focused on his plate. Cameron quietly gasped and looked back at Clay. Bas had turned to stone at his side.

"Jesse was released?" Bas ground the question out.

"How is that possible? I thought they added to his sentence for all that aggravated assault against the police? You should've been notified if he was getting out," Cameron hissed. Clay promptly shut his emotions off and shrugged.

"I saw him the other day when I picked up Charlie from school."

"Did he see you?" Bas fully turned to look at him now.

"Yes. But he didn't approach me. Can we not talk about this right now?" Clay dropped his eyes toward his plate instead of looking at Sebastian's worried chocolate eyes. Bas tilted Clay's chin up to look at him.

"Did you mention it to your bodyguard?"

"No."

"Okay." He turned to his hosts. "Please excuse me for a moment."

He stepped out onto the front porch, phone in hand. Clay watched him from the window, his heart thumping lopsidedly. He was sure Bas was informing the police department of the threat.

"Huh," Cameron said with a huff. "He's not what I expected."

"Me neither."

Clay's family sprawled in front of the television after dinner. Colby was making chocolate chip cookies for Santa while the rest of them watched a Christmas movie. Clarissa had finally crashed from her sugar high and slept, snuggled beside her brother, who was beginning to doze himself.

Cameron suddenly shot up. She winced and held her swollen belly. "Ouch! This kid is trying to kick itself into the world tonight."

"Everything okay, Cam?" Colby popped his head into the living room.

"I'm fine. Just going to use the restroom." She struggled to her feet, Bas offering a hand to help her up. "Thank you—" Cam's eyes went wide as she looked down at the sudden puddle at her feet.

Clay leapt to his feet. "Oh, fuck!"

"Her water broke!" Sebastian hollered at Colby. The father-to-be paled and rushed his wife to the bathroom. Charlie was panicked and fully awake now. Once the initial shock had passed, Clay moved into boss mode.

"Charlie, go get a towel for the floor. Bas, please take Clarissa to her bed. It's upstairs, second door on the right."

Twenty minutes later, Colby was packing his laboring wife into their car. Cam hugged her brother and gave him a laundry list of things to do before Christmas morning.

"I swear to God, little brother, do not fuck this up."

"I got this Cam. The gifts are in your closet. I already sent Charlie to his room. Bas and I can handle the last of the wrapping. Now go get me a new niece or nephew." After buckling his wife in, Colby crushed Clay in a bear hug. "Take care of our girl," Clay told him.

Colby grunted his agreement and hopped behind the wheel, peeling out of the driveway. Clay watched the car's brake lights fade into the distance, his heart pounding from the adrenaline. He let loose a massive sigh, spinning around to go save Christmas and possibly spill his guts to his hot political rival. Time alone with Bas was dangerous since Clay's reckoning in the graveyard.

He found Bas on the floor amidst a sea of wrapping paper, bows, and boxes. Clay smirked and leaned against the door frame, watching Bas meticulously organize gifts by receiver. It was kind of adorable how focused he was.

"Are you going to help me out, or are you going to just stand there and watch?" Bas peeked over his shoulder at Clay, a playful glint in his eyes.

"Yes, sir!" Clay saluted him. "Permission to retrieve the wrapped presents, sir?"

"Granted. Smart ass." A smirk tilted his lips. Clay stuck out his tongue and marched toward his sister's room.

"How many gifts do these kids need?!" Clay tossed his most recently wrapped masterpiece under the nearly suffocated Christmas tree. It was past one in the morning and there were only a handful of gifts left to go. Clay slouched, bracketing his face in his hands while he watched Bas struggle. For a guy who seemed to be great at everything, he was an abysmal gift wrapper. Clay let out a quiet snort as Bas wrapped an obnoxiously long piece of scotch tape around his present. Bas's narrowed eyes shot up to glare at him.

"Pretty sure you used more tape than paper."

"Ugh, why do I suck at this?" Bas pushed the gift away from his line of sight and flopped to his back on the floor. Little scraps of paper surrounded his bulky frame. Clay bit down on his lip to stifle the laugh.

"How about a drink?" Sebastian lifted his hand in a thumbs up and Clay happily hopped to his feet, stretching out his back on the way to the liquor cabinet. He was totally going to drink his sister's good tequila for this. Gathering the expensive-looking tequila bottle and two shot glasses, he shuffled through the wrapping scraps, kicking some out of the way before settling beside the sprawled out Bas.

Sebastian reluctantly rolled into a sitting position and took the filled shot glass from Clay. He clinked his glass against Clay's and downed it. Clay smiled and followed suit, appreciating the burn as it slithered down his throat. Sebastian watched him, reclined back on his palm, empty glass dangling between his fingers. There was a golden sheen to his eyes as he reached over to take the glass from Clay and refill both. He handed the shot back to him and propped an elbow up on his knee.

"To new friends," Sebastian said in his rumbly timber.

"Friends..." Clay whispered, his heart seeming to cleave in two. "Y-yeah. Yes. New friends and the family you make." Clay brought the glass to his lips, but didn't drink, catching how Bas's sleepy smile fell. Sebastian shook his head and took the shot. Clay swallowed his and set the glass beside its twin. They finished the wrapping. Clay was slapping the bow onto his last gift when the tequila reared its head.

"This might be invasive of me to ask... but I'm running on liquor and exhaustion. Have you had many experiences with men?"

Bas froze, his scissors mid-cut. His warm brown eyes latched onto Clay's, and he completed the cut. Putting the scissors down and never taking his eyes off Clay's, he sighed raggedly.

"I fooled around in college. I had a boyfriend, but we never got around to sex. Since then, any encounters I've had consisted of quick hand jobs in a bar bathroom." He shrugged and eyed the liquor again. "Kind of hard to fully enjoy myself after... I worked so hard to stay closeted."

Clay's jaw dropped, and he snatched the tequila, quickly pouring them another round. They drank and Clay poured another. Taking advantage of Sebastian's candor, Clay continued.

"Have you ever been with a different gender?"

"Only once. After High School. It was... depressing." Bas shivered.

"Yikes, can't say I've dipped my toe in that pool."

They fell into silence for a few heartbeats. Clay had begun anxiously cleaning up the trash when Bas suddenly said, "So why the beard?"

Clay looked up in confusion, then belatedly remembered the short, trim beard he'd grown. He scratched the hair on his chin and shrugged. "It's nothing more than a glorified stubble, really. I just felt like it was time for a change."

"I like it." A slow, dangerous smile curled on Bas's face, which immediately heated Clay's cheeks. Bas angled himself so he was directly in front of him. His hand rose and delicately delved into the scratchy hair of Clay's beard. Clay sighed and pressed into his touch. With the addition to the alcohol zinging through his bloodstream, a torrent of words tumbled out of Clay's mouth.

"I want to try. This. You and me. I think I'm ready." Sebastian's fingers stilled and Clay chanced a look. Bas's lips were slightly parted, and the Christmas tree lights glittered in his molten stare.

"You mean. Date? For real?" Sebastian's throat worked in a swallow. A cold spike of dread rushed through Clay. *Oh, shit.*

"It doesn't have to be public if you aren't comfortable with it." He pulled himself away from Bas's halted touch. "We could even wait until after the election. I know this is kind of new for you... but I haven't felt a connection like this since... well, Toby."

"Clay—"

"Or I guess we could just sneak around. Whatever you're comfortable with... I can work with it. Please, just let me try. The cardinal told me it was ok!" *Get a fucking grip, man!*

"Cardinal? Clay, wait—"

"Please, Bas. Give us a chance—"

"Clay!" Sebastian surged forward, slamming his mouth against Clay's, effectively shutting off the babbling. Bas speared his hand through Clay's hair and pulled them flush against each other. They broke apart for a heartbeat and Sebastian chuckled. "Shut the fuck up." He slanted his mouth back over Clay's and deepened the kiss. Desire raged through Clay, and he gripped the back of Bas's neck, nipping at his bottom lip. Bas growled and pulled Clay tighter against him, his hand slipping down to grip Clay's ass.

Clay gasped and pressed his slacks-trapped, hard cock against Sebastian, who he was now straddling. Sebastian groaned into his mouth, feeling his dick rub against Clay's.

"Fuuuuuck." Bas exhaled, reaching between them and yanking at Clay's fly. Clay laughed breathlessly and worked his own hand into Bas's waistband.

"Impatient, are we?" Clay's hand closed around Sebastian's deliciously hot length. Sebastian bucked in his grip, cursing. He'd finally freed Clay's cock and palmed it. Clay muttered a string of expletives and brought their mouths back together. They pumped each other in tandem as their mouths melded. Sebastian's calloused hand slipping up and down his length sent shivers up his spine. If he didn't make him stop, this would be over before it started.

Clay pulled away, earning a groan from Sebastian. He smirked and kissed him once more before standing. Clay's pants hung low on his hips, his dick proudly at attention. Sebastian stared up at him from the floor with hungry eyes. The glistening head of Bas's cock peeked out of the waistband of his pants and Clay couldn't wait to get his mouth on the leviathan that lurked there. Clay pulled him to his feet and dragged him to the guest bedroom at the back of the house. It was thankfully away from the kids' rooms. The last thing Clay needed was to traumatize his niece.

Lust fiercely pounded through his blood as he yanked Bas through the door and locked it behind them with a deafening click. Clay turned his gaze up to Sebastian and smiled wickedly. He pushed his chest, backing him up until the back of his legs hit the bed. Bas fell onto the mattress with a huff. Clay plucked a pillow from against the headboard and dropped it to the floor.

Sebastian's pupils blew wide as Clay knelt between his legs, pushing them farther apart. Clay enthusiastically shucked Bas's pants and underwear, staring in wonder at the nearly ten inches of velvety brown cock resting against his abs. It was positively mouth-watering.

"W-wait, you don't have to," Sebastian moved to pull away, but Clay laid his palm on Bas's broad chest, pressing him down.

"I've been fantasizing about this since I was a teenager." Clay pressed a kiss to the ridge of his cock, making him jerk violently. "Please Bas, let me suck your dick."

# Chapter 26

## Sebastian

He nearly came right then.

"O-okay," he stuttered meekly. Clay grinned devilishly and licked him from base to tip. "Holy shit!" It'd been way too long since his last blow job. If he didn't start thinking about drowning puppies, this was going to end fast.

"Mmm. You taste good." Sebastian's heart thundered. When Clay tightly fisted him at the base, Sebastian groaned loudly. Clay's mouth closed around his cock and greedily sucked him. Sebastian let his head fall against the mattress, a string of curses spilling from his mouth as he curled his fingers in Clay's hair. Clay growled in pleasure from Sebastian's soft tug on the strands, and the vibration zipped through his cock and up his spine.

When Sebastian's tip bumped the back of Clay's throat, his hips bucked. Of course he could deep throat. God was testing his resistance. Clay gagged slightly as he pulled up, his green eyes locked on him. Sebastian got to his feet, twining his other hand into Clay's hair as he sucked him into oblivion. Clay had been leading their pace until this point, but now Sebastian guided Clay's head up and down, faster and faster, fucking his mouth.

Sebastian sucked in a breath, trying to stave off the encroaching orgasm. Clay moaned and whimpered against Sebastian's pistoning hips, the sounds leaving him teetering on a knife's edge. Just before he tumbled over, Sebastian yanked his cock out with an audible pop. Clay's chin and jaw were dripping in saliva, little tears pricking his eyes. He pouted up at Sebastian, licking his lips.

"I wasn't done with that," he harrumphed.

"I don't want to come down your throat," Sebastian rasped. Understanding lit Clay's eyes.

"I haven't prepped."

"I *really* don't care, Clay." Sebastian gripped his glistening length and slowly, torturously, pumped. "Clothes off."

Clay laughed and muttered, "Yes, Daddy."

Sebastian pulled off his sweater and watched raptly as Clay kicked off his slacks and polo shirt. Sebastian chewed on his bottom lip as he cataloged every inch of freckled alabaster skin before him.

"My god, you're beautiful." Sebastian wanted to kiss and lick each and every freckle on Clay's body. He wanted to count them. He needed to figure out what that tiny constellation on his hip was.

"Speak for yourself. You're like... the embodiment of every wet dream *ever*."

Sebastian chuckled and stepped closer. Clay met him halfway, his palm settling on Sebastian's chest. They were finally skin to skin. Sebastian circled an arm around Clay's waist and pressed them firmly together. Thigh to thigh, hip to hip, chest to chest, their hardened cocks trapped between them. Everywhere they touched burned exquisitely.

Sebastian's hand lowered, sliding over Clay's ass, and squeezed. His fingers inched lower still, dipping to his entrance. Clay shivered against him as Sebastian's middle finger prodded there.

"Do you have any lube? I really hadn't thought the night would lead me here," Sebastian quietly murmured against Clay's neck.

"Y-yes, actually. I always keep some in my overnight bag." Clay peeled himself away from Sebastian. Clay flitted into the adjoining en-suite bathroom while Sebastian settled himself on the bed. He quickly dug through his wallet to produce a condom, awkwardly laying it on the side table. When Clay returned, his eyes immediately fell on the foil packet there, and gave Sebastian a lopsided grin.

"Ready?" Clay popped the cap to the lube and offered it to Sebastian. Sebastian nodded and liberally drenched his fingers. Clay giddily joined him on the bed, snuggling beside him. Their kisses started soft, but became greedy and demanding in seconds. They palmed each other as Sebastian's fingers slowly prodded Clay. He started slowly, with one finger, sliding in and out.

He wedged another in, causing Clay to groan in pleasure. Sebastian torturously stretched him while he traced a cluster of freckles on Clay's neck with his tongue.

"*Fuck*. Bas, I'm ready," Clay gasped out between kisses.

"Thank Christ," Sebastian growled against his collarbone. He reached over for the condom and quickly rolled it on, watching Clay flush and pant with desire beneath him. Sebastian notched himself at Clay's entrance, easing in. He released a guttural moan as he inched further, the tight walls of Clay's ass gripping the life out of him.

"Holy crap, you're too big!" Clay's nervous squeak made him freeze.

"Am I hurting you?"

"No! No... well, yes, a little. Just give me a minute to adjust. It's been a while."

Sebastian was stock-still until Clay gave the okay. He pulled out, drizzled more lube on his shaft, and steadily pressed back in. With a few more thrusts, he was fully seated inside him. They both groaned and shivered. Clay rocked his ass against him, signaling it was safe to move. Sebastian wrapped his hand around Clay's cock and pumped in time with each of his thrusts.

Sebastian's head fogged at how tightly Clay's inner walls gripped him. He bit back a moan as he rolled his hips, attempting to slow his movements to keep his orgasm at bay. Clay gasped, his hands shooting out to dig his nails into Sebastian's shoulders. Sebastian's eyebrow quirked up at Clay's response. He quickly repeated the move, earning another shuddering gasp. *Interesting*.

"Oh god, Bas," Clay moaned when Sebastian did it again. A pearly bead of precum glistened on Clay's cockhead and Sebastian wiped it away with his thumb, sucking it into his mouth. "Fuuuuck," Clay ground out, eyes locked with his. "I'm trying to make this last, but you are *not* helping."

"Isn't that counter-productive, Clay?" Sebastian rolled his hips again, his balls tightening. "I'm pretty close," he grunted in a gravelly voice. He thrust again, harder, faster, picking up his breakneck speed from before. He was dancing on the precipice now. Clay covered his mouth, muffling his cries as Sebastian continued to pump him. A wildfire lit in his sparkling green eyes, a silent warning that he was tipping over that edge. Clay's head jerked back as ropes of hot cum splattered across his abdomen. Clay glanced up at Sebastian between fluttering lashes, face flushed and covered in cum. Sebastian tensed for a heartbeat and poured his release into the condom with a quiet roar.

They collapsed in a sweaty, sticky heap, gasping for air between soft kisses. Sebastian wasn't sure who moved first, but they both ended up in the ensuite bathroom stepping into a steaming shower. They lathered and kissed and groped until both were back at attention. Sebastian took him against the tile wall, this time bare. Lost to lust and the headiness of the moment, he lasted all of three minutes.

Utterly spent, Sebastian fell into bed, cuddling Clay from behind. Clay was silent until he erupted into a guffaw.

"I can't believe that just happened," he wheezed between gasping laughs. Sebastian smirked and nuzzled closer, inhaling his specific lemony scent.

"You smell like lemons," he grumbled into Clay's ear. "Have I ever told you that?"

"Oh, really? I guess that makes sense. I use a lemongrass shampoo."

"I've been baking lemon squares, lemon pound cakes, lemon sugar cookies, even lemon meringue pies since Thanksgiving."

Clay went still and Sebastian blanched. *Fuck, I'm going to scare him off.* Clay looked over his shoulder, his eyes glittering.

"Really?"

Sebastian swallowed a lump. "Y-yeah. Is that pathetic?"

Clay turned fully in Sebastian's arms, roping his arms around his waist. His smile was heartstopping. He said softly, "Not even close." Clay kissed him once before nuzzling into Sebastian's chest hair, promptly falling asleep.

# Chapter 27

## Zamboni

The town had turned into a bright cold blanket of ice in the night. Zamboni watched tiny specks of powder flutter to the ground from the bay window.

Krystal hadn't woken for their daily walk, which alerted Zamboni that it must be one of those human "howlidays" they were always chattering about in the cold season. Zamboni huffed and made for the back door. If he didn't open that door, he'd have to pee in Krystal's slippers.

After some scratching and biting at the metal knob, Zamboni was rewarded with a blast of icy air as the door cracked open. He barreled into the snow, quickly relieving himself, before bounding joyously through the fluffy mounds. Zamboni leapt on to a storage container and surveyed the block from his vantage point.

On days like these, when snow fell and humans slept in, the town of Wellsprings was still. All but a quiet chittering. A dark flash darted across the snow, beckoning him to chase. Zamboni looked behind him at the cracked door, huffed out a "borf," promising he'd be back shortly, before vaulting over the fence.

The Siberian Husky raced through the snowy street, hot on a chipmunk's tail. This time, he chased simply for the thrill. He'd call a truce on this perfect day. The chipmunk skittered up a tree, leaving Zamboni to trot down the snow-laden sidewalk alone. His breath puffed into tiny clouds at his snout, but his dense fur kept him warm and dry. He'd always felt at home in the winter. Because of his breed, he suspected.

Sounds of children stirring from the house to his left caught Zamboni's attention. Tongue lolling, he pranced toward the large windows. A small female tore into gifts scattered beneath a decorated pine tree. A young male sat to her right, shaking a package. Zamboni's eyes drifted up to see the two males he'd been seeing all over town. On papers, on the television. Non-Fat Man and Deer Man, both without their previous disguises. They sat cuddled together on the couch, contentedly watching the children.

Zamboni huffed satisfactorily. They must have mated. It was glaringly obvious they'd wanted to before. He turned away from the family and loped down the quiet street once more, making his way toward the town square. The snow, all nondescript mounds jutting from the unmarred icy crust before him, blanketed the gardens.

Wellsprings truly was a glittering gem, but even gems can hide ugliness in the depths of their facets.

# Chapter 28

## Clay

"Are you sure you don't mind staying over?" Clay crossed his fingers behind his back as Bas slung on his jacket.

"I told you I don't mind. I'll grab coffee for us on my way back." Sebastian stooped to plant a kiss on Clay's cheek before heading to his apartment to pick up essentials. He'd agreed to stay and help Clay with the kids until Cameron returned with baby Connor in tow.

"Daaaang, Uncle Clay." Clay shot a glare over his shoulder at Charlie, who slouched against the door frame. "You got it bad."

"Shut up, you little eavesdropper. Go call your parents and thank them for the gifts."

"You should call Santa and thank him for *yours*," Charlie purred, his smile purely feline. Clay waved him off, dodging a hyperactive Clarissa, weaving through the discarded wrapping paper.

Clay video chatted with his sister and the new baby for a while before Bas returned, lemony confections tucked under one arm, a duffle slung on his shoulder, and blessed coffee in the other hand. The kids descended upon the treats like the sugar addicts they were.

"Damn, I should've brought the rest of the pastries. These kids could clear them out," Bas chuckled, wrapping an arm around Clay's waist. His lips hovering at Clay's ear. "When your sister comes back, would you like to join me for dinner?"

Clay flushed, glancing up at Bas from under his lashes. They were really doing this.

"I'd like that."

"How much flour do you think cookie dough needs?" Sebastian dubiously watched as Clay dumped an entire bag of flour into a bowl. "You aren't even measuring anything!" Sebastian snatched the bag out of Clay's hands, appalled. Clay pouted and gave him puppy eyes.

"But I want to help."

"Your niece is more helpful than you," Sebastian scoffed, motioning to Clarissa's meticulous cookie cutting beside them. Charlie snorted a laugh while he mixed a royal icing mixture beside his sister.

"You suck at this, Uncle Clay," Charlie sing-songed, licking the icing from his finger. Charlie flushed furiously and put the bowl down when Sebastian shot him a withering look.

"Unkie Clay sucks," Clarissa giggled.

"Hey! It was *my* idea to make cookies for your baby brother's arrival. Doesn't that count?" Clay glared at the kitchen full of the people closest to his heart. *Dicks.*

Sebastian smirked and handed Clay a collection of measuring cups. "Here. We only need three cups of flour. Can you handle that?"

Clay flipped him off and aggressively scooped the offending flour back out from the bowl. Sebastian chuckled and went back to rolling out the dough for Clarissa's cookie cutting. Charlie sauntered over to his uncle, having finished his icing duties for the moment. He nonchalantly slouched against the counter and whispered, "Damn, he's fine, Uncle Clay. Teach me your ways, sensei."

Clay snorted and flicked a clump of flour at his nephew, "Hell if I know, kid. I'm still trying to figure it out myself." Charlie stared down at the smudge of flour on his black hoodie.

"Bruh! This is my favorite hoodie!" Charlie gaped at him.

"Oh, don't you 'bruh' me," Clay huffed, rolling his eyes. Charlie glared, slammed his hand in Clay's bowl of flour and chucked it right in Clay's face. Clay coughed and whipped his head toward his little shit of a nephew.

"Hey! No food fights in my bakery," Sebastian chided them. Clay glanced sidelong at his boyfriend, swiped the bowl of remaining flour, and dumped it over Sebastian's head. Clarissa squealed in delight and tossed a handful of sprinkles at her brother in retaliation. Charlie hooted and pelted Sebastian with sugar while Sebastian cracked a whole ass egg over Clay's head.

Eventually, there were more ingredients on them than in the actual cookie dough.

One scrubbed down kitchen, ten kid toy assemblies, and one stork delivery later, Clay held his new nephew to his chest, marveling at the tiny human.

"He smells like heaven," Clay whispered in awe. "He's gorgeous. Good job, Sis." Little Connor watched his uncle with rapt attention, tiny fist waving about. Sebastian took the little fist between his thumb and pointer finger, shaking his hand.

"Nice to meet you, Connor."

"Thank you both again for taking care of the kids. And these bomb-ass cookies," Cameron sighed exhaustedly from an armchair, no less than five cookies in her hand. Clarissa was in her lap, clutching her mother for dear life.

"Not a problem, Cameron. Luckily, politics quiet down for the holiday," Bas said. Connor now tightly gripped Bas's finger. Tenderness flitted across Sebastian's face, and Clay felt his heart squeeze.

"Do you want to hold him, Bas?" Cameron smiled kindly at Sebastian's startled look.

"Oh, uh, if it's okay with you, sure." Bas quickly plopped on the couch, awkwardly crooking his arms to cradle the baby. Clay snorted and rolled his eyes.

"Relax, dude," he chuckled, gently placing Connor in Bas's embrace. He softly adjusted the angle of the baby's head and tucked Bas's arms more naturally around the small bundle. Sebastian looked down into Connor's tiny observant eyes, wonder sparkling in his own. Clay's heart sputtered at the sight.

*Oh. My. God. HAVE MY BABIES!*

As if the sight couldn't get any better, Sebastian looked at Clay and a heartbreaking smile bloomed on his face. The room grew silent in the presence of such overwhelming hotness. Even the air held its breath.

Cameron caught Clay's eye and straight up high-fived him in front of everyone.

"Nice job, bro."

Clay snorted at Jade's text and stuffed his phone into his pocket while he checked his reflection one more time. Ever since Sebastian had tipped off the authorities about Jesse, Jade had been on his ass. Even with being distracted by good dick (according to Jade).

Clay shrugged into his suit jacket, carefully adjusting the collar of his turtleneck. He wasn't sure if his outfit screamed "Hi, I am clearly a bottom" or "Hello, I'm a douchebag who un-ironically wears turtlenecks."

Clay frowned and was about to yank off the sweater when his doorbell rang. Well, "douchebag bottom" it was. Grabbing his keys and wallet, he practically skipped to open his door. Bas stood there with a single red rose, a grin on his face. His lips twitched momentarily as he took Clay in.

"Oh," he said, deflating. Clay raised his brows as he took the rose. *The fuck was* that *reaction?*

"Is there something wrong, Bas?"

"I, uh, just thought I'd be dining with Ella this evening."

Clay took a step back. "Oh? And why is that?" He motioned for him to come in while he searched for a bud vase.

"Well, since it's still campaign season and we're going out to eat... I thought it would be easier if you dressed as Ella."

Clay frowned, plunked the rose into the now water-filled vase, and spun to face him. "Easier? Easier for who, exactly, Sebastian? I have a fucking beard, dude."

"C'mon, Clay. For both of us. I thought you liked dressing in drag? If you're uncomfortable with it—"

"I *do* like dressing in drag, but only for fun. I'm not a professional queen. I don't have the right footwear for that."

"That's fine. Forget I said anything. We can just order in food or something... I was only hoping to spoil you for our first official date." Sebastian looked down at his perfectly polished loafers in dejection. Clay took the opportunity to shamelessly objectify him. He wore gray slacks that gripped his thighs scandalously. A cherry red button up with the top two buttons undone, showing some chest hair. His hair was brushed and gelled to the side, with a sliver of hair escaping to tauntingly dangle in his eyes. Holy cockwaffles, he was hot. It'd be a shame to waste that outfit on an evening inside on the couch.

Clay pursed his lips and cleared his throat, drawing Bas's gaze again. "Okay fine. But I hope wherever we're going accepts Uggs, because that's all I have that could pass."

Bas's eyes lit up and nodded emphatically. "Absolutely. Thank you, Clay."

Clay smirked and told him he'd have to wait while he shaved and primped as he sashayed toward his bedroom.

But a sliver of his heart broke off as he left Bas waiting.

# Chapter 29

## Sebastian

Something was wrong.

Clay lifelessly stared into the flames from the hibachi stove before them. He tossed the synthetic locks of red hair over his shoulder, sinking further into the chair. Sebastian found Clay's hand and gripped it tight. Clay wearily looked up at him, offering a watery smile.

Sebastian raised an eyebrow and kissed the back of Clay's hand, mouthing, "What's wrong?" Clay shook his head and attempted to pay attention to the hibachi chef. Sebastian frowned and returned to watching the show.

It was their third date. Their first—a helicopter ride and dinner in a French restaurant—had ended in mutual blow jobs and ecstasy. Their second—a play and a romantic walk through a state park—had ended with more orgasms. He'd seemed fine. Happy. But now, while he fussed with the hemline of his newly purchased dress, melancholy wafted off him.

"For you and your beautiful girlfriend, Mr. Rivera," a waitress said, slipping an appetizer between them, "on the house." Clay stiffened and eyed the plated sashimi.

"Thank you so much," he returned, offering his political smile. She scurried off, and Clay stared back at him. "What's up? I thought you liked Japanese food?"

"I do. Thank you for bringing me. I've actually been wanting to try this place," Clay said with his feminine English accent. They smiled at each other and went back to watching the chef again. Sebastian's heart sank. Clay was definitely upset.

Sebastian stayed quiet. They ate in companionable silence once the chef wheeled his cart away. Sebastian paid, took Clay's hand, and led them to his car.

"What's going on, Clay?" Sebastian drummed his fingers on the steering wheel before pulling out of the parking lot.

"Nothing," he said in his normal voice. He kicked off his heels, groaning as he massaged his foot. "Why do men hate women? These things are torture devices."

"Stop deflecting."

"Fine. I'm sick of the drag, Bas."

"That's fine. We can order in next time so you can be comfortable."

"You're not hearing me," Clay said sharply. Sebastian internally groaned and pulled over, only a few blocks from Clay's apartment. He turned his attention to the fuming man on his right.

"Okay. I'm listening."

"I'm done, Bas."

Sebastian stiffened. "Done?"

"Yes. We're either dating in the open or we're not. It's that simple."

"Well, I already said that after the election—"

"Fuck the election! You know this is about how you're ashamed to be seen with a man."

"You know damn well that this is about Victor and—"

"The inheritance? Yes. I'm well aware of how desperate you are to dangle from Daddy's purse strings. But no. You're a thirty-five-year-old man! If you really wanted to come out, you would have already."

Sebastian clenched his jaw. He wanted to deny it. Tell him how proud he was to be with Clay. To tell him how badly he wanted everything to be out... but he hesitated. He felt the slimy fingers of dread drag down his spine.

"See?" Clay's voice was thick. Sebastian snapped his gaze back to him. "I already did the whole coming-out thing, Bas. Before Toby. And it sucked. I lost half my family because of it. But I did it because I owed it to myself." He shook his head and looked at the hands clasped in his lap. "You're just a coward. And I'm all out of bravery to lend you. I owe it to myself to be happy and right now, I'm not."

Sebastian stared him down. Words escaped him because Clay was right. He *was* a coward. Clay sniffed and shoved his feet back into the heels before opening the car door. "When you're ready to be brave, then maybe we can revisit this. For now... let's just focus on the election. Bye, Sebastian." Clay closed the door and stiffly made his way down the sidewalk, heels clacking. Sebastian watched him turn the corner before he fell apart.

# Chapter 30

## Clay

"So, you only dated this guy for two weeks?" Jade sipped her margarita, judgment heavy in her eyes. Clay winced.

"When you put it that way, it seems pathetic. But the guy was practically closeted still." Clay felt a little gross talking shit about Sebastian. But it wasn't a lie. Still, Clay felt a little like a back stabber. Sebastian deserved his own coming out journey, no matter how long it might take.

"Oh, ick. You definitely don't need that headache." She upended her glass and signaled their friend, Roxy, for another round. Clay gingerly sipped at his whisky and Coke, not feeling up to pounding tequila with Jade.

"That's really the only negative. The sex was great... amazing, actually."

"Hey, don't talk yourself out of it. You were right. It isn't your responsibility to help this guy come out. He should be flaunting you on his arm, not making you wear drag. That's bullshit, Clay."

"Yeah. You're right."

"Ooooh, look over there!" Jade elbowed him sharply in the ribs, pointing at a handsome bear who'd walked into the bar. "Why don't you go chat with him? I know you have a thing for burly men."

"I *do* like bears," Clay huffed and swirled his drink, obviously not interested. Jade laid her hand on Clay's forearm.

"Oh, Clay. This guy really meant something to you, huh?" Jade's eyes glimmered with pity.

"He's the only one since Toby that made me... feel something. But it doesn't matter. It's over."

Jade frowned, opening her mouth, but promptly slammed it shut when she focused on something behind Clay's shoulder. Her hand on Clay's arm tightened before a rumbling voice sounded behind him.

"Can we talk?"

Clay's spine stiffened. A sudden silence stretched through The Hideyhole as Clay built up the nerve to spin around on his stool to face Sebastian Rivera. He wore a scowl on his face, his arms crossed, and he was every bit as handsome as Clay remembered... dammit. Roxy caught Clay's eye from the opposite end of the bar, moving to reach for the baseball bat she kept there. Clay subtly shook his head and inclined his chin to Bas.

"Mr. Rivera, fancy meeting you here. Is it just me, or is this not your typical scene?" Clay asked. A muscle ticked in Sebastian's jaw at the dig. Jade made a tiny gasp of realization at his side. "You'd better leave before you start a scandal."

"Clay. Can we speak—" Bas's eyes darted to Jade and back, "—privately?"

"See ya," Jade nearly shouted at them, snatching her margarita from the bar top, and zooming off into the crowd. Sebastian looked at the stool she'd vacated dubiously before settling down.

"To what do I owe the pleasure of your company today, Mr. Rivera?" Clay focused on his drink, gulping down the rest before turning to Bas.

"You haven't responded to my calls or texts."

"That would be because I blocked your number." Sebastian's brow furrowed. Clay called Roxy over and ordered a Long Island Iced Tea, because why the hell not? Sebastian asked for one also before sliding forward cash for both. Clay glared at him. "I thought we established that I can buy my own drink."

"Clay, please. It's just a drink."

"Oh, like it's *just* a wig?"

"Clay," Sebastian warned. Clay knew he was being stubborn, but goddamn him if Bas thought a drink could fix everything. "I'm sorry."

"Come again?"

"I'm sorry. You were right. I was scared and forced you to be someone you aren't. Ella isn't the person I fell in love with. It was you, Clay." Clay's jaw dropped open just as his blessed alcohol arrived. The two of them sipped their drinks in the quiet as Clay mulled over Sebastian's confession. He turned back to him but saw the steely resolve on Sebastian's face.

"I can't ask you to wait until I figure my shit out. It's not fair to you. But I'm going to keep seeing my therapist. All I'm asking is if you feel at least half of what I feel for you, please don't give up on us yet." Sebastian covered Clay's hand with his, giving it a light squeeze before pushing his drink over to Clay and standing to leave.

"Bas?" Sebastian turned to look at him, something close to grief glittering in his eyes. "Okay." The smile that broke across Sebastian's face nearly snapped Clay's resolve. Sebastian nodded and vacated The Hideyhole. Clay chuckled to himself, realizing that Sebastian had just said he loved him.

"Holy tits on Christ! You banged Sebastian Rivera?" Jade whisper-shouted as she reclaimed her seat. Clay widened his eyes at her and she immediately quieted.

"Now you see the issue?"

"Damn boy, you really know how to pick 'em." Jade swiped the drink Bas had abandoned.

"He said he loved me," Clay said wistfully, tracing the grooves on the bar top. Jade promptly spit out her drink.

"HE SAID WHAT?!"

# CHAPTER 31

## Sebastian

Sebastian stood in the brisk evening air, huddled in his peacoat. He stared down at the gravestone. The sunflowers laid at the base were only slightly wilted. Sebastian gritted his teeth, pacing the row. It wasn't the first time he'd visited this specific plot, but he'd never truly approached or spoke. He was too ashamed of himself for being a coward. But he knew he needed to do this.

Sebastian knelt on the cold ground, pulling the rainbow rubber bracelet from his coat pocket. He traced the letters spelling out *PRIDE.* Unsure where to start, he simply blurted the first thing that came to him.

"You know, the first time I met you, Toby, you handed me this bracelet. You were giving them out to promote the LGBTQ Alliance Club. It's funny, really. I'd just started to question myself and then this guy flounces up to me and shoves a pride bracelet in my hand. It was like the universe said, 'Hey, you're gay, dude.'"

Sebastian vividly remembered the night he'd typed the inevitable *"am I gay"* into a search bar after waking from a wet dream featuring a very naked Chad Michael Murray. He'd lost sleep over it. He'd obsessively deleted his search history and cookies, worried that if Victor ever found out that he'd asked the internet about his sexuality, he would send Sebastian to a pray-the-gay-away camp. When Toby had ceremoniously placed that pride band in his palm during the club fair, he'd winked knowingly and sashayed back to the booth. Sebastian had watched him retreat, fear shooting through his veins. But then a mop of messy red hair cropped up beside Toby and Sebastian's world stopped. He'd suddenly felt... okay.

"I'd always noticed you around school. I was in awe at how you were just so unabashedly yourself. Then, of course, I noticed Clay. How could I not with that wild red head of his? Man, he orbited around you, ass-over-tits in love. And he was even louder about his gayness than you. He was just so goddamn brave. It wasn't long before I had a big ass crush on him."

Sebastian smiled warmly as he remembered the fateful day he'd collided with Clay in the hallway. He'd been trailing behind his teammates, late to lunch as usual. The team had rounded the corner, hooting and roughhousing the whole way. They'd won the away game the previous night and the radioactive joy hadn't dissipated. Sebastian was lost in thought, though. He'd been turning over the conversation he'd had with his mother the night before about what she thought about gay people. Her words hadn't been kind.

That was when he'd slammed into the tiny redhead who'd been rushing out of a classroom. Books and binders scattered around them as the two fell into an ungraceful pile. Sebastian's limbs had somehow become tangled with Clay's, and it was an effort to separate their body parts.

"Shit, I'm sorry. I was late and didn't want to miss out on taco Tuesday," Clay warily muttered, scrambling to gather his things. Sebastian huffed a laugh and helped scoop up some scattered looseleaf paper.

"No worries."

Clay suddenly jolted, glancing up from behind his long lashes at him. The two had shared a biology class, so it came as no surprise that Clay recognized him.

"Oh. Sebastian. Hi."

"Hi, Clay," Sebastian smirked despite himself. He was happy to hear Clay knew his name. Sebastian handed the papers to him and cleared his throat a tad awkwardly. "Are you going to the homecoming rally on Friday?"

"I–oh, um–"

"Yo, Bas!" Jesse's boisterous voice boomed down the hallway. "Is that homo bothering you?"

At the sound of Jesse's voice, Clay stuffed his papers into a book and leapt to his feet. Sebastian grumbled, "Ignore him," before he rose, blocking Jesse's view of Clay.

"Hey! Fuck off, Jesse!" Toby came rocketing out of the cafeteria, rushing to Clay's side. Sebastian's heart sank, but he stepped to the side, striding toward Jesse and company.

"It's all good, man," he said nonchalantly, clapping Jesse on the shoulder, "let's go before they run out of tacos."

Jesse's mouth turned into a stiff line, glancing over his shoulder, unfettered rage dancing in his gaze. Sebastian shook the darkness from his mind. He knew that look had meant danger, even back then, before the bullying had escalated. He turned his attention back to the headstone.

"Well, I guess what I came here to say is that... I'm sorry about the bullying. I know I didn't have an active role in it, but I never stepped in, either. I was afraid. But I know now that's no excuse for standing by like I did. I can't ever take that back. You're gone and I can't help blaming myself."

Sebastian huffed a ragged sigh and crouched down, laying his palm on the hard earth beside the sunflowers. "I love Clay, Toby. I guess I always have. But I can't help feeling like my love is doing you a disservice. And that's something I need to work out in therapy. But Clay... Toby, Clay hasn't let himself fall in love since you died. And I think we can agree, he deserves happiness, regardless if he finds that with me or someone else. But I'd like it to be me. And I hope you're okay with that."

Sebastian stared down at the rubber bracelet dangling from his fingers and slipped it on his wrist for the first time. The lightweight band against his skin was barely noticeable, but its implication weighed heavily. He smiled at it and ran his hand along the top of the gravestone.

"Thank you, Toby. You have no idea how much of an impact you had on my life."

Sebastian turned to leave the graveyard, the setting sun glinting off the scattered marble and granite before him. It was odd how peaceful a ground full of corpses could appear, with birds tittering in the breeze and chipmunks leaping onto tree trunks. Though the light was bright ahead, darkness still lurked behind.

# CHAPTER 33

## Clay

"Mr. Emerson, in your own words, would you please tell the audience why you want to become the Mayor of Wellsprings?" The moderator clutched her clipboard to her chest and smiled expectantly at Clay. He'd answered that in the past several times, but today was the final debate. He knew he'd have to bring the heat today. Taking a deep, cleansing breath, he leaned toward the mic.

"Wellsprings is my home. I love this town." Clay looked out at the sea of cameras and phones. The pride flags stirring in the light breeze.

"My causes are important. Our youth and minorities need to be protected. But you asked why I want to win. At the risk of sounding unprofessional, I'd like to tell you a story. My story."

Murmured whispers erupted in the crowd. Clay risked a glance at Sebastian. His hands white-knuckled the podium as he looked on in shock. Clay offered him a small, watery smile and turned back to the crowd. He shrugged off his suit jacket and hung it over his lectern. He undid the buttons on his cuffs, then rolled up his sleeves, exposing the scars underneath. There was a collective gasp from half the crowd and a quiet, sudden intake from the rest.

"My boyfriend, Tobias, and I were bullied in high school for being homosexual. Those of you who know, know. It got bad. One day, the bullying became too much for Toby and he died by suicide." Clay took a breath, bracketing his hands on either side of his podium. "I found him." His voice was small, away from the mic. But the people heard. More gasps and mutters broke out.

"Let him finish," Sebastian's gravelly voice boomed. Clay didn't look up from the podium. He couldn't look at Sebastian right now. The townsfolk quieted and Clay mustered the rest of his courage.

"Your heart doesn't stop beating when someone you love dies... but it feels like it does. I attempted to take my life that day. But Sebastian Rivera saved my life." Clay's voice warbled with emotion. He looked at the crowd, tears welling. He looked at the man on his left and smiled. "And I hated him for it." Sebastian's jaw muscle ticked, but there was a grim understanding in his eyes. Clay pulled his microphone from the stand and rounded the lectern.

"I blamed myself for Toby's death. If he'd never fallen in love with me, maybe he would've been safe. If I hadn't asked him out in front of his friends, then maybe he'd still be here. If I'd closeted myself more, maybe we could have snuck under the radar."

Clay's voice cracked, heavy with emotion. He averted his eyes from the spectators, blinking away the budding tears. The square was eerily silent, whether appalled from the tale or in quiet sympathy. Clay struggled to get his breathing under control. *This was a bad idea. Too much for a crowd. Too personal.* Each new thought spiraled Clay closer to an anxiety attack.

"None of that was your fault, Clay," the deep velvet of Sebastian's voice rang out through the speakers. Clay snapped his head up to look at him. Sebastian's steady presence grounded him. Clay straightened and looked only at him.

"I thought I was betraying him. For over a freaking decade, I denied myself a relationship because I thought I was betraying Toby's memory."

"I know," Sebastian said solemnly. He smiled sadly at Clay and glanced back at the jarringly quiet crowd at Clay's back.

"Of course, as an adult who's logged thousands of hours of therapy, I know I was feeling survivor's guilt. When I truly understood this, I swore to myself that I'd do my best to prevent something like that from ever happening again in Wellsprings."

He fell silent, staring out at the square. He smiled and was making his way back to the lectern when the first cheers went up. Then, like a damn had broken, the entire town erupted into claps.

The rest of the opening questions were the standard fare. He and Sebastian volleyed back and forth for a bit when it came to the taxes, jobs, and money stuff. Clay was less concerned with budgeting, since Bas was going to fund the anti-bullying program. They'd work the money out like they always had on the council.

Clay subtly rotated his shoulders, attempting to roll some of the tension away after talking ad nauseam about chipmunk conservation. Sebastian was explaining how the casino was backing the Rivera campaign. Clay was still sore about that and forced his attention away from the gorgeous man to his left, surveying the people instead. There was movement at the side of the stage. The Husky, Zamboni, had popped to his paws, body suddenly ridged with tension. Clay raised his eyebrow, trying to catch Krystal's gaze. She was focused on Bas. Clay really couldn't blame her, because *goddamn,* could the man fill out a suit.

Clay watched the dog instead, since he tended to be a flight risk. He figured he could win some hero points if he swooped in to stop the pooch from running off. Again. Zamboni's ears swiveled, nose upturned to sniff at the air. His attention focused on a person in a baseball cap slowly moving through the crowd. The dog's tail stood at attention, his hackles raising. Clay shifted his focus to watch the man in the hat slowly inching his way closer to the stage.

Panic rushed through him. Clay glanced over his shoulder at where Jade stood. She'd been scanning the area, her eyes continually snagging on Marc, but she finally caught Clay's worried gaze. He glanced at the front of the stage and back at her. She jolted to attention and spoke quietly into the earpiece worn by the security detail. Thankfully, from Sebastian's urging, police were milling about the perimeter of the gathered people. A man in a suit approached one and whispered into an officer's ear, eliciting a lot of murmuring into walkie talkies and earpieces.

Clay's eyes found the man in the hat again, now at the front of the stage, right at the make-shift barrier. The man's head tilted up and Clay's worst fears solidified. Jesse smirked cruelly at him, his eyes full of hate. *Shit shit shit shit.* Zamboni's menacing growl was rising over Sebastian's speech now, to where Bas faltered and slowly trailed off.

"I have a question!" Jesse raised a gun, aiming at Clay's head. People screamed and surged away from him, running into the police, who were trying to force their way toward the man with the gun. "Are you fucking this twink, Rivera?" Jesse's question was directed to Sebastian, but his eyes never left Clay.

*Wait. What?* Clay's jaw dropped open. *Rude. I'm an otter if anything.*

Sebastian ground his molars and leaned into the microphone. "He's more of an otter."

Clay threw his hands in the air and sing-songed, "Thank you!" *Stop using humor to hide your terror, Clay.*

"Jesse, put the gun down," Sebastian said gravely. The cops were hedging around the frantic crowd. Zamboni was pulling on his lead, his owner scared shitless.

"You didn't answer the question. Are. You. Fucking. Him?"

Clay swallowed nervously. Why would Jesse want to shoot him? Clay hadn't named him in his earlier speech. Clay scrutinized him. Jesse's attention was now wholly on Bas and Clay realized the gun wasn't pointing at himself, it was tilted toward Sebastian. Clay whipped his head to look at Sebastian, eyes widened in fear. Bas calmly addressed Jesse's question.

"This is a mayoral debate, Jesse. Your question is not appropriate to ask."

Clay looked around frantically. The cops were quickly approaching, weapons drawn. Jade and Marc were at their sides, ready to jump in front of them. Clay studied Jesse closely, noting the steady ticking in his jaw as his eyes grew even darker. *Holy shit. He's going to shoot.*

Three things happened in rapid succession. Clay screamed Sebastian's name, throwing himself at him. An angry snarl sounded, followed by a shout of pain. Then the gun went off.

Clay squeezed his eyes shut, afraid to let himself feel. Afraid that when he opened his eyes, someone would be dead. That he'd been too late to save him. That the man he was in love with was dead. Again. The warmth beneath him rose and fell with a soft chuckle. Clay understood then that he was horizontal, laying on top of someone who smelled of vanilla, sugar and musk. Someone with a solid, warm chest. Someone brushed their fingers against Clay's forehead and pressed their lips where his hair had been parted.

"Clay," the words were dipped in smoke and honey. It was possibly the best sound he'd ever heard. "Open your eyes."

Hesitantly, he did. He came nose to nose with a smiling Sebastian. There was a chorus of shouting and shuffling beyond the podium where they'd landed. Clay didn't have a chance to say a word to Sebastian as Marc and Jade quickly ushered them off stage and into Town Hall. The two guards discussed which room would be the most inconspicuous and secure. The idiots decided on the janitor's closet—the very *small* janitor's closet.

Clay and Sebastian were shoved inside and strictly told to stay put as the door locked behind them. Sebastian fumbled around a moment to flick on the lone fluorescent light. They looked at each other with identical expressions of skepticism

"Who decided either of those two were qualified to be body-guards?" Clay huffed and leaned against a supply shelf.

"I think that was us, actually," Sebastian said with a smirk. He ran his hand through his salt and pepper hair.

"Well, we're morons... are you okay?" Clay busied himself with reorganizing the cleaners on the shelf. They were standing so close. If he wanted, Clay could touch Bas's face just by reaching out his hand.

"Yeah. A little shaken, I guess, but I'm not hurt. What about you?" Sebastian's voice was dropping to a delectable baritone.

"I might have a scraped knee, but your burly body absorbed most of the damage." Clay sighed, abandoned his organizing and dropped his head into his hands. "For a minute, I thought I was cursed."

"Cursed?"

"It's like, every time I love someone, they die. My god, I thought I was going to have to go through that pain all over again," Clay murmured into his palms, voice quavering.

"Clay—"

"I don't think I could survive it again. Who'd ever think it was so dangerous to be a gay man? I mean—"

"Clay!"

Clay jerked his head up, alarmed by Sebastian's tone. He frantically looked around, expecting to see another gun on them.

"Can we go back to what you just said?" Sebastian's face was serious.

"How dangerous it is to be gay?"

Sebastian's lips twitched. "Before that." He stepped closer, breath hot on Clay's face.

"How I thought I might be cursed because everyone I love—oh, shit."

"Oh, shit indeed." Sebastian cupped Clay's bearded cheek. "In case you blocked out my words the other day, I love you, Clay." Clay's breath hitched and he nuzzled into Sebastian's palm, afraid to look him in the eyes. "I know I'm broken. It will take time to fix me, but I'm trying. It's incredibly selfish of me to ask, but would you like to be my boyfriend while I figure this shit out?"

"Bas—"

"You don't have to answer right now. I wouldn't want you to act on something after the trauma we just shared. But... can I kiss you? Because I think I might die if I don't." Sebastian's husky voice sent shivers down his spine. Bas tilted Clay's chin up, forcing him to look at him. Clay audibly swallowed and clutched at Sebastian's jacket, pulling his mouth down to his.

They crashed together, all lips and teeth and tongue. Sebastian pressed Clay into the supply shelf, rattling the cleaning supplies from their place, knocking them to the floor. Sebastian sank his fingers into the hair at Clay's nape, anchoring his mouth to him.

"*Fuck*, I missed you," Bas growled into Clay's mouth. Clay whimpered and tugged him closer. Sebastian palmed Clay's ass, lifting him up and against their growing erections. Against his better judgment, Clay locked his legs around Bas's hips, grinding up and down his length.

"Bas," Clay moaned, dragging his lips up the side of Sebastian's neck. He licked then bit down. Hard. He knew it wasn't the right time to have sex. Not after someone shot at them. Not after Sebastian said he needed to get his head on straight. But his body had other plans.

"Holy shit." Bas gripped Clay's ass tighter. "Are we about to have sex in a closet?"

"Poetic. Isn't it?" Clay slurred his words, heady from lust. They fumbled for their zippers, quickly shedding their respective slacks and suit jackets. Sebastian left his dress shirt hanging open and loose, which was hot as fuck. "Obviously, I wasn't expecting this. So, I haven't prepped."

"Don't care. I just need you." Sebastian spit on his fingers and approached. A zing rushed up Clay's spine, tightening his balls. *Fuck, why was that so hot?* Sebastian lifted Clay's leg, settling it around his hip, and worked his slick fingers into Clay's ass one at a time. Clay cried out while Sebastian's fingers gently rubbed at his inner walls, painstakingly spreading him.

Clay cursed long and slow while Sebastian teased him. In frustration, Clay wrapped his hand around his own granite hard cock and squeezed. He needed to ease the tension. Sebastian pulled Clay's hand away and replaced it with his own, pumping long and slow. Bas's own cock twitched against Clay's abdomen, thick and heavy.

Caressing Bas's engorged dick, Clay greedily slipped his fingers down the velvety length to gently grasp his balls. Sebastian bucked and cursed, losing the slow and steady torture. He plunged his fingers in and out of Clay's ass faster, while simultaneously pumping him with more veracity.

"If you don't get inside me right now, I'll pop your nuts," Clay panted out, still gripping Bas's jewels.

Bas wheezed a surprised laugh and nipped Clay's bottom lip. "Yes, sir." Fumbling with a condom that had suspiciously been in his dress shirt pocket, he rolled it on swiftly.

Then he sank his cock deep inside of him. Sebastian stretched him so deliciously, the pain melding with pleasure. Bas groaned low in his throat, lifting Clay's ass in both of his hands as he punched his hips forward.

"Oh, Clay. *Fuck*, I love you," Sebastian growled out before sealing their mouths together. Clay scrambled to wrap his arms around Bas's thick neck, locking his legs at the ankles around his hips. The friction from their undulating bodies, Clay's cock trapped in the middle, had him riding the edge.

When they broke the kiss to come up for air, Clay gasped out, "Me too. I love you, Bas."

A strangled noise left Sebastian. He turned them, pressing Clay's back against the cool wood door. He pulled him off his cock and slid him up the door to where Clay's head brushed the ceiling. Sebastian looked up at him with a smile, arranging Clay's legs over his shoulders, before closing his mouth around Clay's aching cock.

Clay gasped out a curse, balling his fists in Bas's perfectly coiffed hair as the soul was sucked from his body. "Your mouth is a fucking national treasure."

Bas hummed a laugh, sending ripples of pleasure through Clay's dick and up to his spine. Sebastian braced an arm across Clay's abdomen, securing him to the door while palming his own dick. Clay's breath came in short, ragged pants, watching Sebastian's head bob up and down. He was so close. With a swirl of Bas's tongue, Clay came so hard he lost his vision for a moment.

When the stars ceased dancing in his eyes, he watched as Sebastian greedily drank him down. Bas's guttural shout of pleasure followed, burying his face in Clay's thigh. They looked back at each other in wonder. Bas kissed Clay's inner thigh before lifting him from his shoulders, letting Clay's body drag down his front.

Clay's feet touched the ground, legs still unsteady. Sebastian caressed his face, tracing his cheek bone. With a gentle press of his lips against Clay's, Sebastian pressed their foreheads together. "I'll tell them. I'll tell everyone that I'm in love with you. I don't care what anyone says."

"And your parents?"

"Fuck them. They know I'm gay. They just like to pretend I'm not. They don't matter. You're the only person who matters to me."

"Then, I'd like to be your boyfriend, Sebastian Rivera." Clay looped his arms around Bas's waist. "Wellsprings is going to be scandalized, you know."

Sebastian's lips twitched and transformed into a full grin. "Every political race needs a good scandal, babe." Clay's heart turned over in his chest. Holy crap, he *loved* this man.

A quick rap on the door and Jade's voice—quivering with laughter—came through. "Are you two finally done fucking? Marc owes me twenty bucks and an orgasm."

"Yeah, yeah. Can you two make yourself decent? Apparently, I need to stop at an ATM," Marc said in a gruff chuckle.

Clay and Sebastian stared at each other and burst out laughing.

# CHAPTER 32

## Zamboni

The sounds were hurting Zamboni's ears.

He wasn't sure why the humans had all gathered in the town square, but there was a lot of fanfare. A platform was constructed beside the site of the chipmunk's den. Many humans had been gathering around the area in the past week, roping areas off as females with clipboards hustled about. Krystal hadn't let him off leash while the *conservationists*—whatever that meant—were around.

Now Zamboni laid down on the stage at Krystal's side. He rested his head on his paws, pinning his ears flat against his head as the crowd's volume surged. Two males strutted on the stage. By their familiar scent, he knew it was the two men who'd chased him. The burly deer man and the bearded man, though his beard appeared more real this time.

Zamboni also recalled seeing the pair close on the howliday from the window. But something seemed stiff in their gaits as they regarded each other. He lifted his head and scented the air. Strange. They no longer smelled mated. Zamboni popped to his paws. No, that couldn't be.

The men shook hands once they met at the center of the stage. Despair wafted from both of them. Beard Man's mouth twisted down into a brief frown. He quickly wiped the sadness from his countenance and turned to smile at the crowd. No way. They'd obviously mated at some point. There were the faintest traces in their scents. Zamboni whined sharply and rocketed away from Krystal, pulling the leash from her hand.

"Zambo, no! Goddamnit," Krystal hissed at him. Zamboni bounded up to the pair, wrapping his lead around them similarly to how he'd done months prior. The men collided with each other. Zamboni barked in triumph, eliciting a chorus of laughter from the crowd. Zamboni leveled his gaze at them and lolled his tongue out in a mocking grin. *There, you idiots. Take a hint.* He huffed a borf at them before Krystal crashed into him, wrestling his leash from the idiots.

"Oh my gosh, I'm so sorry, guys."

"It's fine, Krystal. In fact," the bearded one said, crouching down and offering his hand to Zamboni, "I haven't properly introduced myself. I'm Clay."

*Oh! Paw!* Zamboni plopped his paw into his palm and tilted his head. *Treat now?*

He didn't get a treat, but Clay patted the space between his ears. Clay smiled at him, his earlier discomfort no longer visible. He pointed to the Deer Man behind him.

"That's Sebastian." Zamboni turned his gaze up to the big man. Sebastian was smiling fondly, but his eyes were on Clay. Zamboni huffed at him. Sebastian's eyes shifted to Zamboni and grinned lopsidedly.

"Hey there, troublemaker."

Zamboni barked and wagged his tail before Krystal apologized again and pulled him off stage. They stood at the sidelines beside the stage, but not anywhere Zamboni could get into trouble. He panted, more nervous about being closer to the crowd.

The humans suddenly hushed when Clay began to speak. Zamboni tuned him out, watching the faces of the people instead. He sampled the air, trying to get used to the overwhelming smells of so many people in one space. Zamboni's ears pricked up when he caught the tail end of an odd smell. He wasn't sure what it was, but something about it made his hackles rise. He inhaled again, deeply. There! It was a smoky smell. One he often smelled around the town when the hunting season was upon them, but that time was a way off yet. Zamboni growled low in his throat as realization hit.

Someone in the sea of people was carrying a gun.

# CHAPTER 34

## Sebastian

J esse was back in custody.

He'd been promptly tackled by the police that night, right after mayoral candidate Zamboni broke free from his owner and bit Jesse's gun wielding arm. If it hadn't been for that dog, making the shot go wide, someone could've died. That damn dog was totally going to win the election. Who didn't love a hero?

Sebastian tugged on the knot of his tie for the fiftieth time. He was standing in the wings of the stage, watching the town council address the crowd. Tonight was the big night. They'd tallied the votes and a new mayor would be announced after their appreciation speeches. Across the stage, at the opposite end from him, Sebastian spotted Clay's auburn hair. Their eyes met, and they quickly shared nervous smiles.

If Sebastian was being honest, he hoped neither of them won, knowing the position would only cause animosity in their fledgling relationship. No, Sebastian wasn't worried about the results. He was nervous about what he was about to do. A sudden clap on his shoulder made his spine jolt.

"Easy, son. Just me," Victor grumbled. "You're nervous? That's unlike you."

"Yeah well... this is a life-altering announcement."

Victor nodded sagely and offered his son the barest hint of a smile. Essie joined them, looping her arm through her husband's.

"We're so proud of you, Sebby. Regardless of the results. Right, honey?" Essie nudged Victor with her elbow. But his father's smile was gone. *Whoops.*

"Yeah, guys about that." Sebastian took a deep breath before continuing, "I'm in love with Clay Emerson."

Essie gasped, dropping Victor's arm and holding her hands to her mouth. Victor only frowned and shook his head.

"This nonsense again."

"No, Dad. Not nonsense. I'm gay. Get the fuck over it."

"Please welcome Sebastian Rivera to the stage!" the emcee announced cheerfully. Applause followed and Sebatian stared down at his father, smirking, before striding toward the podium.

"Sebastian, don't you dare." Victor's soles pounded after him and Sebastian rushed to the microphone before Victor could intercept him.

"Good evening, Wellsprings! How is everyone tonight?" More cheers went up, and Sebastian smiled broadly. He glanced a peek at Clay and winked.

"So, I have a bit of an announcement." Sebastian removed the mic from the stand, much like Clay had at the previous rally, and rounded the podium to address the crowd.

"I've recently started a relationship." Some scattered claps and a stray wolf whistle sounded. "I know this isn't directly related to politics, but…" Sebastian glanced behind him and saw Victor fuming at the edge of the curtain. He smirked at him and looked over at Clay.

"Mr. Emerson, would you mind joining me on stage?" Clay's shocked face turned rosy as realization lit. His mouth gaped as he dragged his cute little ass to Sebastian's side. Clay smiled up at him, looking insanely kissable. If Sebastian really wanted to scandalize the town, he supposed he could, but the people needed baby steps.

Sebastian grinned at Clay and twined their fingers together, bringing his attention back to the awestruck, silent crowd. He directed his lopsided smile at them until a woman shrieked in the back and started chanting "kiss, kiss, kiss." Soon the whole of the square was echoing it. Clay tugged on Sebastian's hand, once again claiming his attention.

"We should probably give the people what they want, huh?" Clay's eyes smoldered, and he licked his lips in anticipation. "No tongue though, we wouldn't want the boomers in the front row having heart attacks."

"Oh, no. We wouldn't want that," Sebastian rumbled before sealing his mouth over Clay's in a searing kiss. Shrieks of joy echoed around them. The two laughed before turning to the crowd.

"Tonight's results are inconsequential. Whoever wins will bring their best for the town of Wellsprings. And those of us who don't win will work behind the scenes to do all we can to make this town the best it can be."

Sebastian grinned at the crowd, hooking his arm around Clay's shoulders. "That about sums it up for my closing remarks. Mr. Emerson, the floor is yours." Sebastian lowered the mic to Clay, arm still firmly wrapped around his shoulders. Sebastian doubted he'd ever stop touching him now.

Clay chuckled exasperatedly and said into the mic, "Well, how the hell do I follow *that*?"

# Chapter 35

## Clay

Clay paced the corridor of the VFW—the only event space in Wellsprings—while he waited for the votes to be finalized. Tanya scowled at him from behind her tablet.

"You're making my anxiety spike, Clay," she hissed.

"Sorry. I just... there's so much hinging on this." Like his entire career and budding love life. If Sebastian won, Clay would seriously have to consider breaking it off, knowing his pride would get in the way. Bas didn't deserve that. At least the anti-bullying program would get funded, even if Clay's life imploded. Small victories and all that.

Across the hall, the Rivera team was waiting for the results. Sebastian had been quickly sequestered by his father after the speeches. Cameron kept poking her head in to check on her brother's pacing.

"Clay, we should be practicing your victory and concession speeches, not," Tanya said, gesturing to his frantic pacing, "whatever this is."

"Uncle Clay?" Clay's head whipped around at Charlie's voice. His nephew looked dapper in his pink blazer and white button up, holding out Clay's speeches scrawled on index cards.

"Oh, Charlie, thanks. You certainly took your time grabbing these, huh?" Clay smirked at him but was greeted with a sassy eyebrow raise.

"Excuuuuse me? I've been standing here for ten minutes while you had your panic attack."

"Ah."

"Do you want to talk about it?" Charlie glanced at Tanya. She harrumphed and screeched, "Five minutes," before returning to their party room.

"Oh god, is a Gen Z'er about to lecture me?"

"Yes, you poor misguided Millennial. You're bugging out because if Sebastian wins, you won't be able to separate the job stuff from the romance stuff."

"That's alarmingly accurate."

"Okay, well, it's simple. A job is a job. Your life will mean nothing if you aren't happy. Does Sebastian make you happy?"

"I think... I mean, yes. I love him."

Charlie grinned and pulled Clay in for a quick, tight hug before stepping back, straightening Clay's lapels. "Then don't let him go, Uncle Clay."

"You're pretty wise for your age, huh?" Clay ruffled his nephew's pink hair, much to his chagrin. Charlie swatted him away, restyling it with his fingers.

"You can thank TikTok for my education."

"Clay," Tanya gasped, slamming the door to the party room open, "it's time."

Clay's stomach was in knots. He forced a smile and held his note cards in a death grip. Cameron stood beside him, gripping his arm with one hand and cradling her baby with the other. His brother-in-law gripped his shoulder on the opposite side while Charlie and Clarissa huddled in front of their little family unit. They all stared at the huge monitor dangling above the room with local reporter Nancy Fennington grinning at them.

"We're just waiting for the town council to submit the final counts. Oh! It seems like we have our new mayor!"

Mort, the oldest living member of the council, shuffled his old bones up to Nancy with the results shaking in his hand. "Hi Mort! Do you have the name of our new mayor?" Nancy angled the mic down to him. Mort smiled at the camera.

"Yes, I do. Congratulations, Mayor Zamboni!"

The hall went silent until Charlie erupted in laughter. Mort explained how the town council had been running things without a mayor for years and would continue to make any necessary decisions for the town. Clay tuned the rest out. He glanced down at his sister, a mix of shock and elation mixed on her face.

"Go," she whispered, giving his arm a squeeze. He grinned unabashedly, turned, and ran from the room, succession speech forgotten.

Clay slammed through the doors of the Riveras' party room and into chaos. Victor Rivera was raving at his son and team about how unacceptable the loss was. Sebastian's face was red with anger. Marc was hovering near the shouting and caught Clay's eye. He gave a subtle shake of his head. *Not a good time.*

"Sir, as I was saying, the council would like to extend an invitation to Mr. Rivera. Mr. Emerson is already a member, and they can both serve the town this way," Jensen, one of the lead council members said to a fuming Victor.

"How can you let a *dog* win? Is that even legal?"

Sebastian finally exploded. "Enough! Dad, you're being unreasonable."

"Like hell I am! You saw the numbers! You lost to a gay and a dog. You're a fucking disgrace," Victor spat. Essie, who'd been beside Bas, whipped her head to her husband. Bas opened his mouth, but Essie placed a hand on her son's chest.

"Our son is not a disgrace. The only disgrace in this family is *you*, Victor."

Victor's eyes narrowed on his wife, lines of tension on his face. "Me?"

"Yes. It's you who keeps me from sharing my culture with my son. You who denies Sebastian his choice of lover." Essie turned to Bas, regret and love in her eyes. "I'm so sorry I allowed this pig-headed man to control me for so long, *Mijo.* Everything you do makes me proud. Love who you love. Do what you love. I will always support you." She cupped Sebastian's cheek, pulling him down to place a kiss on his forehead before turning back to her husband. "I want a divorce."

Essie spun on her heel and strode away. Victor, aware of every eye in the room, pulled in a panicked breath and chased after her. Cold shock doused the room. Clay whispered a *damn* to himself, earning a glance from Bas. Once Sebastian saw him standing there, the hurt and confusion disappeared from his eyes. He smiled, stepped forward, and pulled Clay into a bone-crushing hug.

"Sorry we lost," Bas murmured against his ear, lightly grazing his teeth against his lobe. Clay shivered and squeezed him tighter. "I'm not."

A throat cleared to their left. Their heads snapped up, seeing Jensen awkwardly hovering at their side. "Sorry to interrupt. Mr. Rivera, are you interested in the council seat?"

"Ah, that." Sebastian disentangled himself from Clay and held out a hand to Jensen. "I appreciate the offer, but I have other plans." Jensen nodded sagely and shook Sebastian's hand before flitting out of the room like his pants were on fire. Who could blame him?

"What other plans?" Clay tilted his head up at Bas. Sebastian smiled widely, cupping Clay's cheeks.

"Guess we'll find out," Sebastian growled before slanting their mouths together.

# CHAPTER 36

## Zamboni: One Year Later

T he humans were so much nicer now. When Krystal and Zamboni had their morning walks, all sorts of people stopped to talk and pet him. He got treats at every store they passed. Then the vet—ugh, the *vet*—said he'd gained weight and Krystal started giving him a different kibble. He didn't like it, but the treats made up for it.

The store where they were going was one of his favorites. The big deer man, Sebastian, owned it. It smelled of sugar and yeast and lemons.

"Only one treat from the bakery, Zambo. I really don't want to get berated by Dr. Dickhead again," Krystal murmured as she yanked open the door to the bakery, the tinkling of bells signaling their entrance.

Sebastian's head swiveled toward the door, throwing her a grin before turning back to the customer he was serving. Clay was standing at the opposite end of the display case, chatting with Sebastian's mother. Clay caught their entrance from the corner of his eye, spun, and launched himself at Krystal, wrapping her in a hug.

Since his owner had met the couple, they'd grown to be friends. Zamboni often followed her to what she called *Bridgerton* Watch Parties at the men's shared apartment. Sebastian would sneak him popcorn while Clay and Krystal squealed over something on the television.

"Clay, you look like a pride parade vomited all over you," Krystal huffed out in amusement.

"That's clearly the point, Krystal. I had to go all out for Bas's first parade." Clay winked dramatically and blew a kiss to Sebastian, who rolled his eyes while ringing up his customer.

"As long as you don't make me wear something that crazed. It's assaulting my corneas," Sebastian grumbled once the customer left with their bag full of treats.

"You seemed to have no problem with the rainbow thong I put on this morning," Clay challenged, crossing his arms.

"*Madre de Dios,*" Mrs. Rivera mumbled and scurried into the back. Sebastian winced.

"Sorry, Essie," Clay called after her.

"Can you please stop traumatizing my mother?" Sebastian pulled out a tray of quesitos, Krystal's favorite, and threw three in a bag. He also pulled out the jar of homemade dog biscuits. *Treat!*

"I will, as long as you stop being a little bitch and at the *very* least wear the rainbow shorts I got you."

Zamboni wagged his tail viciously as Sebastian tossed his apron and rounded the display case, bag and treat in hand. Zamboni danced in circles before planting his rump on the tiles and lifting his front paws. *Treat?*

"Ugh, I'm so over this new begging thing with him. Like, how pretentious," Krystal said, taking the bag from Sebastian with a quiet thanks.

"Well, he *is* our esteemed mayor." Sebastian placed the treat on Zambo's nose. "Stay," he said, dragging out the word. *Treat, treat, treat!* "Okay, go for it!"

Zamboni moved his nose in a flash, snapping his jaws down as the treat dropped. The peanut buttery oats were Zambo's favorite. He licked any crumbs from his muzzle, hoping for another taste.

"I really hope he loses weight. Otherwise, I'll have to find a different vet. I literally almost punched him last time."

"Oh! Dr. Dickhead?" Clay slung an arm around Sebastian's waist and leaned in to inspect Krystal's bag. She rolled her eyes and broke off a piece of quesito for him.

"Yes, him."

"Wait... isn't there only one vet in Wellsprings? What about your schooling? Aren't you graduating soon?" Sebastian plucked the sunglasses from Clay's head and put them on. Krystal groaned and deflated.

"Yes... I'll have to look for a clinic in one of the neighboring towns. I *cannot* work with that guy. Major ick." Zamboni watched with rapt attention as she bit into a pastry.

"Hold up," Clay grinned devilishly. "Didn't you say he was hot as hell?"

"I..." She glared at him. "Yes. He is. But it doesn't fix his personality."

Clay and Sebastian grinned and glanced at each other knowingly.

"Whatever you two idiots are thinking, stop." Krystal huffed, spinning on her heel. "Have fun at the parade. C'mon, Zambo."

Zamboni popped to his paws, snuffling his wet nose into Clay's hand and then Sebastian's, eliciting quick pets before bounding after his owner.

# Epilogue

## Sebastian

He was wearing the stupid rainbow shorts. They rode up mid-thigh, showing off his muscled legs. Sebastian had a suspicious feeling that had been Clay's plan all along considering how much he was staring. He also had on the black mesh tank top Clay had begged him to wear… and the rainbow Chucks… and the rainbow feather boa.

He looked like a goddamned idiot. But Clay beamed when he saw the ensemble and Sebastian found he didn't care. Until they left their apartment to find Jade and Marc gawking at them in the hall. Marc laughed so loud that their elderly neighbor had popped her head out to glare at them. Sebastian swiftly punched him in the gut and apologized to Mrs. Wheelen. He carted their rag-tag group of fashion crimes from the building and directly into the limo he'd rented.

Jade immediately queued a playlist on the Bluetooth sound system while Marc opened the sunroof, popping his head out and whooping. These buffoons had clearly been pre-gaming. Jade blasted a Taylor

Swift song and lounged in her mashed-up outfit of yellows, pinks, and blues. Marc finally sat down as the limo driver pulled away from the curb and dished out the complimentary hard seltzers from the cooler. He wore a black T-shirt with ALLY in big rainbow block letters. *He* got to wear normal length gray cargo shorts with a pride flag bandana tied to a belt loop. Sebastian scowled at Clay for making him wear the tiny shorts currently pinching his balls. But Clay was busy, conspiratorially glancing at Jade.

"Do you have the goods?" He had to shout it over Taylor singing about being the problem. Jade smiled fiendishly and pulled a bulk bag of fun size Skittles from the giant reusable shopping tote she'd smuggled in. Marc good naturedly lowered the volume, receiving a cutting glare from his girlfriend.

"Should I even ask what you need those for?" Sebastian eyed his boyfriend nervously. Clay grinned at him and pecked him on the cheek.

"Don't worry, babe. You aren't a part of my scheme this time." Clay plopped the skittles on the seat beside them and stretched out his legs. Sebastian greedily took in Clay's bare calves, his gaze traveling up to his matching rainbow shorts. They hugged his crotch deliciously but fit him better than Sebastian's. He wore a pink tee with the rainbow script reading *Sounds Gay, I'm In!* The rainbow heart shaped sunglasses were teetering on his head as he cracked the seltzer Marc had tossed him.

Jade handed Sebastian a seltzer. "Bas, are you sure Essie can handle the bakery a couple days on her own?"

"Yeah, she should be just fine. Since the divorce money came in, we could hire a part-time baker. We've been doing pretty well, too."

"I'll say. I'd assault a toddler for your chocolate croissants," Marc said a tad too seriously. Sebastian smiled. He was proud of that recipe.

After losing the mayoral race, Sebastian had worked with Essie to release his trust and together they opened *Panadería Rivera*—after funding Clay's program, of course. Essie taught Sebastian to bake traditional Puerto Rican desserts and handled the finances since she'd been CFO of Victor's company.

Victor.

The thought of his father still gripped his heart in a vise. He'd run with his tail between his legs after the spectacle he'd made. Sebastian hadn't seen him since. Neither had his mom, except for the settlement meeting. Essie assured him that Victor had looked like shit.

Clay squeezed his knee, offering a sympathetic smile, undoubtedly knowing where his mind had gone. Sebastian gripped his hand. Clay's gaze wandered down to their joined hands, lingering on the rainbow bracelet around Sebastian's wrist. He'd obviously questioned why Sebastian had insisted on wearing the circa 2004 wristband. Sebastian couldn't tell him it was because the ridiculous baby shorts didn't have a pocket for the small velvet box in his bedside drawer.

"Holy shit. My eyes are fucking burning," Sebastian growled, stepping into the boisterous crowd of color. Clay snorted and tugged on his arm, following Jade.

"Who would've thought Sebastian Rivera was a fashion snob?"

"Smart ass!" Sebastian chuckled, swatting at Clay's aforementioned ass. He glared at him over his shoulder. Marc was keeping pace beside him, giving him sidelong glances. He gave Sebastian a thumbs up when Clay's attention was elsewhere and slinked off to prepare.

Sebastian was instantly sweating through his mesh top, not solely from the crush of bodies. They finally reached the edges of the parade, Jade handing the Skittles over to Clay.

"Okay, right before the dance troupe finishes, we join the end moves, and then throw the Skittles," Clay instructed Jade, their eyes sparkling with mischief.

"Clay! You said no schemes," Sebastian mock scowled at him.

"Actually, I said *you* weren't a part of my scheme. You could be if you wanted. But you don't know the moves."

"Are you sure no one's going to tackle you two?" Sebastian's heart was racing. Of course, he knew about Clay's little surprise. He, Jade, and Marc had been talking for months to plan around Clay's crazy. And Sebastian *did* know the moves, thank you very much.

"Bas, they reached out to *me*. You realize we're semi-famous gay icons, right?" Clay haughtily looked over at his boyfriend, actual annoyance in his tone.

"Okay, okay. So, the moves... are they hard to learn?" The smile that lit up Clay's face was worth the hours of torture Jade had put him through those nights Clay stayed late at the council. Newsflash: Sebastian was an abysmal dancer. Clay quickly listed the moves off, demonstrating swiftly. As if Sebastian would pick it up from that display alone.

"Got it?"

"Uh," Sebastian blinked at him before Clay squealed. The troupe was quickly approaching. Sebastian audibly swallowed and swiped the sweat from the back of his neck. Marc miraculously appeared at their side, excuse popcorn in hand. His best friend patted him on the shoulder and whispered encouragement in his ear.

The dance troupe was before them, shuffling into place. Clay excitedly stuffed bags of Skittles into each of their palms, instructing them once again on when to throw the bags. Sebastian smiled at him. *God, I love you.* It was suddenly their cue and the three of them rushed into the center of the group, flowing into the team flawlessly. Clay was surprised Sebastian had kept to the beat and grinned wildly, clearly believing himself to be a dance guru.

Just as they were supposed to make their big finish, the dancers all spun away from them, circling their trio. Clay faltered, looking around in confusion at the change in choreography. His cheeks flushed, and he looked back at Sebastian in confusion only to find him on one knee. Clay gasped, and the music quieted. A few wolf whistles rang up from the spectators. Clay looked at Jade, who smiled and handed Sebastian the microphone, slipping into line with the other dancers.

"Bas..." Clay's voice was thick with emotion.

"Clay," Sebastian began, slipping the rubber bracelet from his wrist and holding it between them. He tucked Clay's hand in his free one before continuing. "I've kept this bracelet for twenty years. Because it was given to me the day I first met you." There were muttered "awes," and "oh my gods," around them. "Toby gave it to me on a day when I'd been questioning everything I ever thought about myself. Then I looked up and immediately fell in love with a dorky little redhead. Twenty years I closeted myself. Twenty years I've secretly been in love with you. And I can't go one more second without you being my husband."

Tears tracked down Clay's face and glittered in the corners of Sebastian's eyes. "Clay Emerson, would you do me the honor of marrying me?"

Clay full-on sobbed and nodded, unable to speak through his emotion. Sebastian grinned and slipped the band on his wrist, roughly pulling him into a kiss. Screams and applause erupted around them.

Confetti cannons blasted from the dancers and rainbow beaded necklaces were tossed through the air.

"Don't worry, the ring is at home. Some loser made me wear these booty shorts with no pockets," Sebastian whispered into Clay's ear.

"Oh, I know. I found it last month. It's perfect." Clay kissed him again. "And your ass looks fan-fucking-tastic in these." Clay swatted Sebastian's aforementioned butt with a giggle. The music swelled around them and the dancers shuffled back into formation. Clay's head snapped up, and he tossed his Skittles bags into the surrounding spectators.

"Taste the rainbow, bitches! I'm getting married!"

THE END

# Acknowledgements

Thank you so much for reading *Politics Suck*! Please endure my gushing, because this book would never exist without the support of my readers, family, and friends. Thank you for sticking around. I'm super excited for you to read Krystal's story next!

Now on to Sebastian and Clay, the two little idiots of my soul. Their love story is full of heavy topics, but I felt it was important to still discuss it. Besides, we're all a little broken and so are our heroes. For anyone who has struggled with bullying, ostracization, and predjudices, you are seen and valued. Please never stop sparkling.

Huge thank you to my parents for never letting me give up on my dream and for genuinely being my most excited readers... I'm sorry the word cock was used so much this time around.

To my anime buddy and best otouto ever, this was for our little BL loving hearts. Charlie was a living tribute to our insanity. Love you, bro.

To my beta/ARC team, thank you so much for your support and endless insight. This book would never have gotten off the ground without you all.

To my editor, Heather Andrews, thank you again for your valuable guidance and countless words of kindness. Also, no, tsundere was not a typo, I'm a shameless otaku.

Finally, to my husband, remember how in the acknowledgements of my last book I couldn't promise I wouldn't ask you more sex-related questions? Well, at least I'm not a liar. Thank you for being my very first reader and suffering through the sexy bits. I swear I'll write a fantasy for you one day...but you know there's going to be spice. A leopard can't change it's spots, babe.

**ROSEMARIE DILLON** lives in New York with her family. When she isn't working her nine to five, you can find her writing in her closet, reading romances as her children dogpile her, or actively trying to keep her toddler from jumping off the highest ledge he can find. She is the author of *The HR Nightmare* and the *Wellsprings Rivals* series.

## VISIT ROSEMARIE DILLON ONLINE

RosemarieDillon.com

@rosemariedillonbooks